SOME MEN DESERVE TO DIE

A Jack Damen, M.D., Mystery

L.C. Larsen

Copyright © 2021 Lars C. Larsen

All rights reserved

This is a work of fiction. Some scenes were developed from the author's experiences during a career in medicine, and certain long-standing institutions, agencies, and public offices are mentioned, but all characters in the novel are imaginary and any resemblance to actual persons, living or dead, is coincidental.

*TO MY WIFE AND CHIDREN, PATRICIA,
JENNIFER, LARS, AND ELIZABETH, FOR THEIR
NEVER-ENDING LOVE AND SUPPORT.*

CONTENTS

Title Page	1
Copyright	2
Dedication	3
Prologue	7
CHAPTER 1 – Four Months Later: The Crash	9
CHAPTER 2 – January: The Beginning	20
CHAPTER 3 – 5 North	36
CHAPTER 4 – A Benefactor's Request	46
CHAPTER 5 – The Assignment	53
CHAPTER 6 – Faces of Love	63
CHAPTER 7 – Despicable	68
CHAPTER 8 – Anita	78
CHAPTER 9 – Hell by the Bay	86
CHAPTER 10 – Coffee at the North Shore	111
CHAPTER 11 – First Trip to the Windy City	120
CHAPTER 12 – Volunteers	134
CHAPTER 13 – The Sisters	143

CHAPTER 14 – The Coroner	152
CHAPTER 15 – Inside the Solishe Estate	159
CHAPTER 16 – Thirty Years Ago	170
CHAPTER 17 – A Team in the Pits—and Revelations	174
CHAPTER 18 – Realization & Danger	188
CHAPTER 19 – Going Forward and Reaching Back	194
CHAPTER 20 – Choices	198
CHAPTER 21 – Holding On	209
CHAPTER 22 – Anita's Decision	214
CHAPTER 23 – Help Needed	227
CHAPTER 24 – After the Crash: Black, White, and Gray	231
CHAPTER 25 – What Jasper Knows	246
Epilogue	263
Acknowledgement	271
About The Author	275

PROLOGUE

It was a harsh winter day on Chicago's North Shore, worse than most, with early afternoon temperatures sub-zero, snow in the air, and a driving wind that stung the face like small needles. Under the gray and gloomy sky, a small cluster of luxury cars and SUVs gathered in the driveway of an impressive estate, reflecting the wealth of those who came to offer condolences to the widow of Carlton Solishe.

Mrs. Solishe's longtime male aide, dressed immaculately as usual, opened the front door as people arrived and accompanied them to the sitting room where Anita Solishe, "Annie" to those who knew her well, received them. Dressed in widow's black, she met with visitors for several minutes and then guided them to the adjoining family room where comfortable seating and restrained refreshments awaited, promoting discussions of the day's events and just-learned details regarding Carlton's death. Between visitors, a few close female friends would filter back into the sitting room to soothe her loneliness and worsening grief. If only they had known that Annie felt better today than she had for the past fifteen years. Carlton Solishe had been unpleasant to casual acquaintances, ruthless and amoral to his associates, and despised by those who knew him best. At last she was free.

CHAPTER 1 – FOUR MONTHS LATER: THE CRASH

It was 3 a.m. and light from a full moon beamed across the Pamlico River and between the pines at Kirby Island, where Emmi Pollard was running down a gravel road. She was scared, not of the gunshots that woke her—she grew up around firearms and hunted on her family's farms —but that the man she loved was dead.

Seven hours ago, while on an after-dinner walk with a neighbor, she watched a taxi from Raleigh turn into Jack Damen's driveway. It was not good news: the other times when Jack couldn't drive himself, he'd been exhausted or having a nervous breakdown.

"God," she whispered through her footfalls, "please let him be alive."

Sue and Fred Donegan were peering out the window in their kitchen as Emmi sprinted into Damen's drive. Weekly renters from Chicago, they'd been enjoying Kirby Island's peaceful aura until last evening, when a cab stopped at the empty house next door and dropped off a stranger who was staggering, muttering, and pointing toward the sky. He appeared intoxicated and disoriented but somehow managed to unlock the front door and stumble into the house.

The weathered barn-wood walls muted the new neighbor's jabbering, but his wailing kept the Donegans awake until after midnight—they told the police later that he sounded 'like an abandoned dog." After a train of thundering obscenities and explosions from a large-caliber handgun shocked them from sleep, they called 911 and hunkered down in their home, too frightened to go outside and investigate.

Like all the cottages on flood-prone Kirby Island, Damen's was perched atop tall wooden posts with the living area ten feet above the ground. Emmi bounded up the front steps and through the unlocked door. She found him on the back deck.

Her scream sent chills through the Donegans and everyone in the neighborhood who heard it.

A lone police cruiser was parked in Damen's driveway at 9 a.m., deserted by the vehicles of the State Trooper and city deputy who'd responded to reports of a murder on Kirby Island, the high-end neighborhood on a tiny peninsula two feet above river level. Prized by waterfowl hunters for a century, medical professionals, lawyers, and wealthy others had invaded over the past fifteen years and built homes on stilts for weekend sojourns among the locals and nature. Shootings of humans were uncommon there; ducks and geese weren't so lucky.

The Hooper County Sheriff, J.D. Daughtry, was inside talking with Emmi, enjoying the coffee she'd brought from her place and brewed on Damen's French press. He'd known Emmi since middle school, and like many of the boys in their community, had a crush on her through high school. The youngest of the three Pollard sisters, she seemed made for the beaches on the Pamlico River: brown-blonde hair that hung over her shoulders, tanned skin that looked better without makeup, and a figure that attracted gawking adolescent male classmates like a magnet.

After twenty years and being up half the night, she's still beautiful, J.D. thought. He shook his head to remind himself there was business to be done.

Setting his empty cup down, he said, "I know this is hard on you, but would you run through everything again? I need to make sure I get my report right."

Emmi grimaced with pain, "Come on, J.D., do I have to?" Her eyes welled up and she took a deep breath. "Okay, okay… I ran over from my house after I heard the shots—they came from the direction of Jack's place, and nobody hunts at that time of night around here. The house was empty—," she closed her eyes, "except for an empty fifth of Scotch in the kitchen and his coat and shoes on the floor in the dining room along with some chairs that had been turned over. It looked like a bomb had gone off, all sorts of stuff thrown around, and there was a smoky smell." *I won't tell him I was worried that Jack had gone crazy,* she thought.

"Then I found him on the back deck. He was lying on his stomach, in the moonlight and not moving. Shell casings and blood were everywhere… The pistol was still in his hand, and I thought he'd killed himself." She lowered her face and tears trickled down her cheeks. "I lost it until I saw him breathe… The blood was from where his head hit the coffee table when he fell, and after I made sure the bleeding from the cut on his head had stopped, I was able to look around. That's when I saw the burnt Bible…and his open wedding album." *I can't stand this*, Emmi thought, *after all we've been through, he still loves Beth so much.*

She sobbed and covered her face with her hands.

I just want to hug and comfort her, thought J.D., *but I've got to stay professional here*. He gently handed her a facial tissue.

"Thanks, J.D." After wiping her eyes and face, Emmi continued, "The wood chips on the floor from the edge of his roof toward the moon told me the rest of the story: he was having another PTSD attack, got drunk, and tried to shoot God, who he believes took Beth away from him." She closed her eyes and her shoulders began to shake again.

J.D. felt sorry for her. *Here she is*, he thought, *a smart-as-hell lawyer, beautiful, saved her family's agricultural business, and has all the money she'll ever need, but she can't have the one thing she wants: the unconditional love of this screwed-up physician who will always love another woman more than her*.

He recalled what a family scandal it was after high school when Emmi chose to attend Southern University rather than follow her sisters to Grace University, where women received a traditional southern education in social skills for marriage to successful men. Freed from parental yokes, she earned her undergraduate and law degrees at Southern, met and married Don McLaughlin, an insurance salesman, and was happy for the first time in her life.

They settled in the City of Medicine, and on weekends, would drive to the Pollard family cottage at

Kirby Island to enjoy the river and slow pace of life. Friends dropped by, and there'd be neighborhood fish fries where homeowners, new and old, could get to know one another better. It was at one of these where Emmi and Don met Jack and Beth, and they hit it off and developed a close relationship that was uncommon among couples. Then, it all fell apart: Don got cancer and died a miserable death over eight months, followed by the Damens' divorce two years later.

Emmi looked up and interrupted his thoughts. "J.D., we love each other and have talked about getting married, but it will never work as long as he feels the way he does about Beth—he just can't let go, even after *six years!*" *Dammit, he seemed to have coped with his feelings about her and why she divorced him, but he hasn't*, she thought, *and I'm not sure he'll ever get over the guilt he feels about her being institutionalized in that nursing home. I just need him to get past it all!* She hesitated, "And these spells he has, they circle back to her or times in his life I can't relate to. I mean, he's told me he did some bad things in the military but clams up when I ask about them."

J.D. nodded but didn't say anything. He knew how hard it had been for Emmi, an independent, successful woman, to find a local man who wasn't intimidated by her. Pollard Farms had been on a downward financial spiral following her dad's retirement despite the best efforts of her sisters and their spouses, so after Don died, Emmi returned home to run the business. She took control and turned everything around by the time the Damens' divorce was finalized, but in the process became starved for male companionship. So, she decided to pursue another project: Jack.

One of Emmi's faults, J.D. thought, *was that she confides in her old high school friends too much, including my wife, Laura, who filled me in on everything—how Emmi convinced Jack not to sell the house on Kirby Island after Beth divorced him, and why it wasn't long before they were seen walking hand in hand on the beach.*

The seduction trap backfired, though, and instead of having a stable relationship focused on meeting her physical needs, she fell head over heels in love. Her friends watched as things got serious, and J.D. decided to check Damen out beyond his fancy doctor degree. It took him three months and a good friend in the State Bureau of Investigation to get a glimpse into Damen's service record, and from the limited look he had, the current situation wasn't surprising.

Emmi said, "J.D., what are you thinking?"

"Nothing...I'm just glad he's alive," he lied.

She continued, "This spell is worse than the others —he's never gotten his gun out before or been violent with his religious beliefs... He has a psychiatrist at Southern and I have a call into him and should hear back soon. If he wakes up before then, I'll give him one of the sedatives we have left over from the last attack; it's been less than a year, so they should still be good.

"Sometimes I don't know what to do, whether I should walk away from him or stay. I mean, I don't need him to support or take care of me, but we really enjoy being together, and I like taking care of his place when he's off being a doctor at Southern."

Her voice caught and lowered to a near-whisper. "Working through these attacks is hard, but at core he's a good man."

She's always been a rescuer, J.D. thought, and recalled when Emmi and some high school friends tried unsuccessfully to save an ailing bottle-nosed dolphin that swam up the river. There's no question that she'd keep trying to save Jack because that was who she was…and, she loved him.

"Emmi, we all like him. He's given free medical care to most of our families through the years and probably nothing will come from this, so don't worry. I'll come back in a few days and talk with him. Make sure you let his psychiatrist know how serious this episode was, and that I'll have to put Jack in jail if he pulls out a gun during another one.

"As it is, he scared the living bejeezus out of those folks renting the Shepard's place. That's my next stop, to convince them there'll be no danger to them staying there... That reminds me, go through the house and take any firearms you find over to your place and keep them there until Jack's back to normal." *Normal*, he thought...*right*.

Emmi said, "I will, for sure, this morning." She gave him a hug and stepped back. "Thanks for being such a good friend—you and Laura are always there when I need you."

She hesitated. "I don't know why he got violent this time. In his other attacks, he has collapsed inward, like he lost all his strength. He's fighting something in this one. The Christmas holidays and when we've been together since then were fine, but I haven't seen him in about a month. The last couple of times we talked on the phone, he was quieter than usual, and when I asked if something was bothering him, he said he was consulting on an insurance investigation near Chicago and wasn't allowed to talk about it. He did say, though, that it had become complicated and was getting to him—and a couple of days later he shows up here all messed up. Whatever was going on, it must have been terrible..."

J.D. left after completing his report, and Emmi began the long process of putting Damen back together. For three days he came out of the bedroom for meals, ate without saying a word, and went back to bed. She fed and washed him, held him close when he screamed in the dark, and cried softly as he grieved.

There was an unexpected interruption one morning, when an FBI agent based in Raleigh came by the house to inquire about a man who had recently gone missing in Chicago—he said Damen was the last person to have seen him. Damen's PTSD symptoms were still severe, and the agent left forty-five minutes later after watching him shake and repeat, trance-like, that the man had "seemed fine." He didn't return.

The Pamlico River was a gentle healer, with its tidal currents and soothing winds, and timeless acceptance of all things human. And Emmi was there, day after day, for three weeks—her accountant managed the business while she was gone—and nursed him back, wanting nothing in return except his smile that promised better days ahead.

Then, one morning, Damen awoke with a clear mind, looked around the sunlit bedroom, and stretched under soft, thin covers. Emmi was sleeping next to him. The sweating, frequent awakening, and worst of all, total-body shaking that accompanied his memories had taken a night off. Sleep had been restful, at last.

His PTSD attacks had been rare since leaving the service, only two in the years before his divorce.

After Beth left him, however, they had been happening every year, most near the anniversary date of their divorce; each time he prayed he wouldn't kill himself or someone else. They seemed to be improving, until this one, when events, horrific memories, and a recoiling conscience demolished his mental firewalls.

He closed his eyes and thought about January and how it began.

CHAPTER 2 – JANUARY: THE BEGINNING

The snow ant phenomenon occurred every four months at Southern Medical Center Hospital, when medical students and first-year residents arrived in pressed white coats as medical teaching teams changed and the newcomers disrupted everything for a few days. Although Southern's residents and students were among the smartest in the nation, learning to apply the universe of facts acquired in medical school to sick patients wasn't easy.

So young and they don't know shit, mused Adele Sharpson, R.N., as she watched them scurry between patient rooms, faces painted and hair combed, chomping at the bit, and totally lost in the helter-skelter of hospital patient care.

There are four medical teams assigned to the

North floor of the hospital, and as Charge Nurse, it was her job to record the occasional spikes in patient deaths and medical complications that occurred while faculty physicians and upper-level residents on each team instructed their junior residents and students how to care for patients. *I just hope there aren't too many screw-ups this time around*, she thought, then relaxed. Fortunately, Dr. Jonathan "Jack" Damen was back, and she'd never seen spikes for a team he supervised. Her job had just gotten easier, if you could say that.

Outside, the "City of Medicine" was coming to life with groans and screeches of sanitation trucks and other traffic echoing in the January air. People rising for work, families for school, society's night workers scurrying home, and the homeless clearing from doorways—the signs of a new day. A fresh, cool breeze tickled noses and invigorated sleep-dulled senses. Inside the hospital, 5 North also awakened but with a far different sensation.

Yecch, this floor stinks, thought Sharpson. *Three patients have diarrhea and it smells like something crawled up inside them and died, then vaporized into the halls.* She chuckled as newbies veered away from the assaulting doorways, as if walking around puddles, while trying to act like experienced doctors. Medical care in the hospital was dirty business and they wouldn't be pressed, painted, and combed much longer.

Sharpson was working the graveyard shift, 11 p.m. to 7 a.m., and the teams had arrived an hour before sunrise for work rounds. She knew that despite these and other "sunrise surprises," they'd come to love the early morning stillness and quiet, perfect for moving from patient to patient without getting distracted by nurses, medical colleagues, or families wanting to talk with you. There would be time for that during teaching rounds.

Other than "the three Ps"—poop, problems with the new electronic medical record, and patient care disagreements with her nurses—work rounds went well for the four teams. As they left to meet with their faculty teachers in the Hospital Annex, all Sharpson could think of was getting home to sleep. How to manage the assertive female newbie, the unpretentious one with the glasses who seemed to know what she was doing, would have to wait until another day.

Thirty minutes later, Team 2 gathered around a conference room table to meet Dr. Damen for teaching rounds and to discuss the team's next two months. Hefty doses of coffee ratcheted up their eyelids and jump-started muscles sleepy from the day's early start. Black, muddy, and strong enough to grow hair on a rock, it was a welcome stimulant, especially this first morning.

Dr. Joon Kim, the third-year resident on the team, sniffed his half-filled cup and gazed around the table at the doctors and students he'd be supervising. Damen demanded excellent patient care 24/7 and didn't tolerate careless decisions. They had worked together during last year's flu epidemic and Kim knew Damen respected him, but serving as a senior resident leading this medical team was going to be a different ballgame. Fortunately, the team seemed to be a good one, and with Julie McKenzie as his second-year resident and backup, things should be fine…assuming they would be able to get along.

Kim looked at the tall, slender, dark-haired resident lost in her own world. *She's a one-off*, he pondered, *smart with looks like a pouting runway model, but her pout isn't an act*. Her deep green eyes seemed to reflect a suppressed anger and sadness within, and although they worked well together this morning, he had doubts about their future relationship.

Across the table, Julie McKenzie, MD, stared into her coffee and twirled her hair while thinking of last weekend's blind date. *What a dud*, she mused. *Another former-jock, mama's boy who thought I'd cuddle up, fascinated by hearing about his favorite sports team–*

Her thoughts were interrupted by a giggle eruption among the first-year residents.

Drs. Michelle Lewis and Mark Mestule were cackling about an interaction with a nurse that morning, Lewis's strong southern drawl infusing her laughter. Raised in a rural Eastern North Carolina town, the sole daughter among three children of a Baptist minister, Lewis had an accent that could easily be mistaken for lack of intellect. If Kim hadn't told her, Julie never would have guessed Michelle graduated first in her medical school class at Johns Hopkins.

God, she's plain, McKenzie observed. *Uncolored brown hair pulled back in a ponytail, metal-rimmed glasses, and hazel eyes that move like they're stuck in glue. With a makeover, she could be cute, but I don't think it matters to her. Mestule is her best friend at Southern, but he's married and out of circulation, so it must be a brother-sister thing... He's kind of hot, though, and it would definitely not be platonic with me*, McKenzie thought as she looked at Mestule.

Lanky, with the casual appearance associated with prep schools—bow tie, combed dark hair, and a quick wit and smile—Mark Mestule had been raised in Connecticut, graduated from Harvard Medical School, and chose Southern for his Internal Medicine Residency because he felt it was the best in the country. Gifted like Michelle, he was attracted to her intellect, and after a few home-cooked meals at his house, they'd become close friends.

Michelle and Mark's wife, Jean, had bonded right away; she was a soothing sounding board for conflicts that arose from the demands of residency training. The long hours of studying and treating patients' life-changing illnesses were taking a toll: rather than paying attention to Jean and his two-year-old son, Mark used most of his time at home for sleep and mental recuperation. Michelle understood this, and her empathetic support was proving vital in preserving Mark and Jean's marriage, as was Mark's devotion to the family.

Joon Kim watched as Julie eyed Mark. He knew that stressed medical residents, male and female, were vulnerable targets for romance seekers during periods of marital strife or discontent. Affairs among physicians, nurses, and hospital staff were common causes of divorce—and as leaders of health care teams know, of serious interpersonal dysfunction within their teams.

This is not good, he thought. *Although whatever two consenting adults decide between them is okay in most situations, if she starts moving on him, I'll have to talk with her. It would be a fling for her and a marital catastrophe for him, and I'm not willing to pick up the pieces and run team damage control in addition to everything else I have to do for our team and patients.*

Kim knew that if everyone stuck to the script and their medical responsibilities, the team would be fine. McKenzie was smart and so was Mestule, and Michelle was smarter than both of them and seemed to be a rock, so he hoped any interpersonal drama would be kept to a minimum and they could meet Damen's expectations for the medical care they delivered.

But we may not for other reasons, Kim speculated, as his eyes caught the debris field on the other end of the table.

The remaining members of his team, the two fourth-year medical students, Nyquim Berry and Holly Jones, were chin-wagging and sharing a fruit-chocolate breakfast bar. Notes, crumbs, and pens were scattered in front of them and their backpacks tipped on the floor behind—internally Kim sighed: the scene reminded him of bohemians in a bus station cafe. They had shared with him their worries about having zero patient-care experience and Damen's high expectations, and said they'd work hard to make sure no medical issues fell through the cracks. However, the picture they painted at the moment showed nothing but sloppiness.

There was another issue bothering Kim: in the hospital, medical students must process and integrate reams of information into diagnostic and treatment plans, and some had not been able to do this. It became obvious when they were unable to formulate appropriate care plans for patients, and their resident supervisors needed a massive amount of time to correct this. Worse, when those efforts were unsuccessful, the students required re-direction into non-clinical careers such as medical informatics or pharmaceutical drug development. It had happened last year with a student Kim supervised, and the negative impact on how the team functioned—teaching, patient care, communications—was huge.

It would be unusual for lightening to strike again this soon, but these two were peculiar, and Kim and McKenzie would have to keep a close rein on their medical care until they learned how they thought and what made them tick. And given their backgrounds, it was unclear if Berry had the spine, or if Jones had the heart, to love medicine and embrace the self-improvement and work needed to succeed.

Unlike most students at Southern Medical Center, Berry and Jones had been drawn to medical careers late. Berry, the first male in his African-American family to attend college, majored in Physics but realized he would be happiest in a profession where he could serve people face-to-face. Against the advice of his professors—they couldn't envision the skinny-as-a-rail, bespectacled, shy student as a physician—he applied to the best medical schools in the country and was accepted at Southern, where he continued receiving straight "A" grades; recurring comments from professors praised his analytical skills while noting his reluctance to engage in unpleasant, but necessary, discussions about his performance.

Holly Jones loved History and English in college and wanted to be a university History professor, then an English professor, and after losing interest in these, an attorney. But fate intervened and her mother got breast cancer—the fourth woman in the family in two generations to be afflicted—and it was discovered she and her daughters, Holly and a sister, were carriers of the BRCA1 genetic mutation that increased the risk of developing breast cancer and other malignancies. After months of soul searching, Holly decided to dedicate her life to cancer research; she changed her college major to Premed, graduated summa cum laude in five years, and was accepted into Southern Medical School. Considered "quiet and a good student" by most professors, others had commented she appeared "bored," and "about to fall asleep" when dealing with topics unrelated to cancer.

Joon Kim was brought out of his reverie by a firm knock on the door. It opened.

The team fixed their eyes on the man who entered the room: mid to late 40s, black hair, long white coat, broad shoulders, a face seasoned by experience and past exposures to the elements, and a presence of strength that blurred the lines between blue-collar and academic medicine settings. Joon watched McKenzie's expression change as she sat up straight; Lewis's and Jones's faces also reflected female admiration. Mestule and Berry shifted in their chairs, sensing the subtle physical threat of a dominant male. He was different than other doctors at Southern.

"Good morning, I'm Jonathan Damen. Most folks call me Jack and I hope you'll call me 'Jack' or 'Dr. Damen,' whichever matches the situation and your level of comfort."

He shook Lee's hand and sat down at the table. "Joon, it's good seeing you again. I'm glad you're Chief Resident on the team." Damen looked around. "Who else do we have here?"

The self-introductions were quick and, in a few cases, revealing. McKenzie leaned forward and flashed cleavage over her scrubs top, more so than with other male teachers, and Michelle Lewis blushed when Damen reminisced about Johns Hopkins and Dr. Cecil Adamson, a mutual professor that was still there. Damen took everything in, explained his expectations to the group, and concluded with the Henry Ford approach and the Mother Rule.

"The patients on our service have serious and complicated diseases, and to manage them, what I call the Henry Ford approach to medicine seems to work best: outside of hospital politics and matters of the heart, nothing's complicated if broken down into its component parts. Simply put, complex patients do better when underlying causes are identified and addressed at admission and every day thereafter until discharge. And, it doesn't happen without focused effort and hard work. You have to be a detective and think, think, and think some more about your exam findings, lab and radiology results, diagnoses, and so on. Break everything down to the basics, collect more information, take time to think about it, and then decide what needs to be done. That's when you act, not before. We'll be spending a lot of time every day reviewing each patient's medical problems, old and new, and what to do about them. Any questions?" Damen hesitated. "None? OK."

Looking at each member of the team, he continued. "The Mother Rule means you should give patients the care you'd want for your own mother regardless of their socioeconomic status. When people are sick, they're vulnerable and scared and the least we can do when poking, prodding, and sticking them is to treat them with dignity and consideration for their individual needs.

"One of the finest physicians I've ever known treated all patients the same whether they were homeless or the CEOs of Fortune 500 companies. You're bright as hell or you wouldn't be here, so the real challenge will be truly *caring* for your patients. Providing the correct medical care is a given here at Southern. Providing the correct medical care *in the best way* sometimes is not, usually because we get rushed and are in a hurry. You need to do the right things, for the right reasons, in the most humane way, all the time, even when nobody's watching."

He tabled his hands and let his eyes travel around the group. "Questions about any of this or the next two months?"

There was total silence. The team instinctively knew they were lucky in their placement—this guy was different than most teaching attendings, confident like the others but with an apparent honesty and humaneness not often seen in the ivory towers of academic medicine.

When no one responded, he said, "OK. Joon, where and when would you like to begin rounds?"

Kim had anticipated the question. "How about 5 North, room 525, in fifteen minutes? I'd like to review a few things with the team before we start."

Damen stood up. "Fine. See you there."

After Damen left the room, Joon raised his voice to address the team with other details that would serve them well. "Damen's for real—smart as hell and really cares about patients. He doesn't tolerate sloppy work, you know, inattention to detail and that sort of thing. And God help you if you ever lie to him. Just remember that when he asks you something, he either knows the answer or is pretty close to it. He's super inquisitive—like a detective on steroids—and has an unbelievable memory and ability to come up with diagnoses that no one else had considered. That's why he's the personal doctor of many of the faculty here; he's just damn good.

"And one final thing: like the rest of us, he's not perfect. I've heard from residents ahead of me that there are times when he has to leave the school for a few weeks—some kind of PTSD—he just disappears and then comes back good as new."

Michelle Lewis glanced around at everyone and said in a soft voice, "I'm embarrassed to tell you guys this, but when I learned he'd be our faculty teacher, I called a friend a year behind me at Hopkins to ask around, you know, to learn what he was like when he was there—I figured with luck someone might recollect him.

"When she talked with some of the older professors, they all remembered Damen—he's sort of a legend. Almost all of them said he was the best medical student they'd ever had, you know, super smart and hard working. And there were stories about him, including one about Dr. Adamson that everyone seemed to know—God, I hope I didn't turn too red when he mentioned him."

Mestule said, "You did," and laughed.

Lewis pinkened and continued. "So embarrassing... Dr. Adamson's still a professor there, and I shouldn't know about this. Anyway, this is what she said."

Years ago, Adamson enjoyed humiliating faculty colleagues he didn't like whenever they gave conferences about their complicated patients. He would read all he could beforehand about the medical issues involved and then ask difficult questions. If they didn't know the answers, he'd attack their credibility in public during the conference—it was a rotten thing to do.

Adamson was presenting at a large Morbidity and Mortality Conference one day about a patient of his that died, and in summing up, said the cause of death couldn't be determined. The room was quiet, and Damen's hand raised.

"Yes?" Adamson asked.

Damen said, "Given his electrolytes and vital signs, I wonder if the problem could have been primary hyperaldosteronism?"

This hadn't been considered, and as soon as Damen mentioned it, most of the people in the room realized this was a possibility.

Caught off-guard, Adamson became defensive and condescending. "I thought someone like you might say something, but there's no way to establish *that* diagnosis."

Damen said, "Actually, there are three ways the

diagnosis could have been made," listed them off, and sat down. Everyone knew he was right. The place exploded—people screamed, threw papers, and laughed as Adamson received a huge serving of humble pie.

After things quieted down, he shook his head, chuckled, and said, "Dammit, Damen, I think you might be right," and the place went wild again.

Adamson hadn't humiliated a faculty or student in public since then, and he and Damen later became good friends.

Lewis continued. "My friend also said the faculty were surprised when Damen went into a Family Medicine residency in Rochester after he graduated—they didn't even have one at Hopkins—he told them he wanted to learn how to care for young and old patients with all types of illnesses. Three years later, he returned to Hopkins and joined the Internal Medicine Residency, became a Chief Resident, and stayed on as an Endocrine Fellow, where he began his research in thyroid disease."

She sure learned a lot about Damen for this rotation, Kim thought, *stuff I've never heard about. I wonder what she has unearthed about me. Or McKenzie.* He interrupted her. "Sorry, Michelle, we have to get going," and he added to the group, "Southern recruited him after fellowship, and his research since has been ground-breaking—that in addition to giving unbelievable patient care." He hesitated. "These months will either be the best you've ever had, or the worst... Let's go to 5 North."

CHAPTER 3 – 5 NORTH

Four days before Team 2's meeting with Dr. Damen, Shirley Forlein looked out her living room window and saw Camilla Oliver watering the lawn next door. Camilla's auburn hair was neatly combed, but her makeup was too thick and lipstick strayed around her lips. There were two other problems: it wasn't her lawn and she was nude.

Shirley called her husband to take a look. "John, Camilla's at it again—she's watering Perez's yard, and she isn't wearing any clothes. I wonder where Bill is…"

John said, "Call and see if he's home so he can come and get her; it's forty-five degrees outside and she might get sick. If he's not there, we'll have to call the police—remember July when she was fishing for sea bass in the middle of the road and hooked me in the chest with that damn lure as I tried to take her home? And she took off running? Christ, that hurt... Never again!"

Thirty minutes later, passersby walking to the afternoon basketball game watched a scrum of soaked city police load a blanket-wrapped-Camilla tortilla into a van. It had been quite a battle, Camilla screaming and waving the hose like a showering assault rifle before being tackled and wrestled into submission.

She was taken to the hospital emergency room for evaluation where she cursed the medical staff, claimed to be kidnapped, and demanded to see her lawyer. Medical evaluation confirmed toxins from her ailing liver had accumulated in her brain. Unfortunately, this was nothing new.

Being the wife of a Southern University department chairman, Camilla hosted frequent dinner parties and extended after-dinner gatherings for students, faculty, and visiting dignitaries. She had been born with a natural inclination toward alcohol and enjoyed large amounts of wine and tequila, a 24/7 passion that had plagued her for the past seventeen years. The ensuing cirrhosis was destroying her liver.

She'd been admitted to Southern Medical Center innumerable times for intoxication over the past decade, and legions of medical students and residents owed their knowledge about managing alcohol abuse and liver failure to her. It had become customary to admit her to the hospital floor where the medical and nursing staff knew her best—5 North—and she was sent there again.

Now, after four days of treatment, she was coherent, realized where she was, and allowed the nurses aides to dress her without screaming, biting, and scratching. All seemed to be going well except her serum sodium level was slowly increasing, and the previous medical team had not addressed it.

Team 2 was assembled in the hallway outside her room when Damen joined them and began teaching rounds.

He said, "Who's caring for Mrs. Oliver?"

"Mark, Holly, and me," said Julie McKenzie, as Kim, Lewis, and Berry watched on.

Noticing Holly's disinterest, Damen said, "Holly, why don't you give us a quick summary of Ms. Oliver's hospital course and medical problems?"

THAT got her attention, Joon Kim chuckled to himself.

After Holly's summary, Damen asked her, "Why do you think the serum sodium is increasing?"

Holly said, "Maybe she's getting intravenous fluid that contains extra sodium, or perhaps a medication with sodium in it."

McKenzie interrupted. "She's *not* getting too much sodium; I checked that out. So ordinarily, this would be due to a water deficit, but we've reviewed her fluids—what's going in and coming out—and they're OK. There must be another cause."

Turning to the rest of the team, Damen asked, "What do the rest of you think? Joon, please hold your thoughts." There was no response and he continued. "Michelle, what about you?"

Michelle said, "Mrs. Oliver is on a medication that has diarrhea as a side effect and she might be having more diarrhea than anyone appreciates."

McKenzie's eyes narrowed. "I *just* said her fluid balance is fine."

Damen looked at her, nodded, and said, "All right." He turned to Michelle. "How do you think we should proceed from here?"

Averting her eyes downward, she said in a soft voice, "I'm not sure."

Wow, Damen thought, *these two are going to have fun together*—he understood the interpersonal dynamics involved and that Michelle had ceded to McKenzie's alpha position on the team. He said, "There's one piece of the puzzle missing here. Have we talked with Mrs. Oliver about the number of stools she's having? I'm also worried she's losing fluid in her stools—let's double-check with our patient."

McKenzie jutted her chin. "OK, but we reviewed the nursing notes three times and they documented only four to five stools daily, and not large ones."

They entered Camilla's room and found her in a chair next to the bathroom, eyes yellow, face dull-beige and wrinkled, and hair Medusa-like. An intravenous line dangled out the sleeve of her bathrobe. She looked tired.

Damen shook her hand. "Mrs. Oliver, I'm Dr. Jack Damen, the new faculty teacher on our service taking Dr. Hardy's place." He gestured toward the team. "You've already met the others here. Holly has told me about you and says you're doing well except for an increased concentration of salt in your blood, what doctors call "sodium." It's nothing serious at this point and we're working to figure out what's causing it. How do *you* feel you're doing?"

"Well, Dr. Damen, I think I'm doing fine except for this damned diarrhea. It seems like I'm going all the time."

"The nursing notes say you're having four to five bowel movements every day. Is that correct?"

"Four to five? You're kidding! I've been on the commode every hour or two and I can't leave this chair or I couldn't get back to it. My rear end is sore and swollen up like a baboon's."

McKenzie thought, *Fuck, Damen is going to think I'm dumber than hell*. Mestule and Jones stared straight ahead and Kim bit his tongue—he knew humility in medicine comes one slice at a time through missed diagnoses, medical mistakes, and unexpected outcomes, and it was beginning for Julie, Mark, and Holly.

Damen said, "I'm just wondering why the nurses haven't recorded them."

Camilla said, "The nurses are busy with other patients and I don't want to keep bothering them every time I go into the bathroom…it would be all the time. I mean, it's like when they give you that stuff for a colonoscopy: you do your business again, again, and again, all watery, except this hasn't stopped."

"Well, we're going to change one of your medicines and you should notice an improvement in the next twenty-four hours. Are there any other problems you feel we need to address today?"

"Yes, there's something I'd like to talk with you about. Alone."

"That's fine. Julie, why don't you and the others step outside and figure out how we can fix Mrs. Oliver's diarrhea and elevated sodium? I'll be out in a few minutes."

"Got it," said McKenzie. She wondered what Mrs. Oliver needed to talk about that couldn't be shared with the team.

Damen sat on the edge of Camilla's bed as the team left and closed the door. "So, how can I help you?"

"Doc, even though I've only known them for a few hours, these young doctors don't seem to get it. I've been working on my alcoholism for years. It's just *so* hard. I've been to inpatient and outpatient rehabilitation programs, but I can't stay away from the booze. My liver's being killed by the stuff and I'll probably die from it. The problem with your doctors, especially Dr. McKenzie, is that earlier this morning they treated me like a dreg of society.

"It was dark, they asked a few questions, then left without telling me how I'm doing or anything. I heard them laughing in the hall afterwards and knew it was something about me. It's as if, because I'm an alcoholic and keep coming to the hospital with liver problems, I don't count as a person. And by the way, you're the first doctor who's asked about the number of BMs I've been having. They didn't, that's for sure."

It was a pitfall for many new physicians—this time our young doctors, Damen rued, *where they got absorbed in the impersonal world of diagnoses, lab results, treatments, and hurried pace of necessary work and forgot that meeting the psychological needs of patients was necessary for good medical care.* He knew those needs often hinged on how patients interpreted the language and behaviors of their healthcare providers, and a lack of compassion and careless language within earshot of patients could not be tolerated. *Our team will learn from this episode. Right now, however, I need to tend to Mrs. Oliver's hurt feelings from being devalued by McKenzie and the others.*

Ten minutes later, Damen came out of Camilla's room and reviewed the team's plan for her. He said, "This is spot on, really good work. Let's get it going right away."

Adhering to Vince Lombardi's feedback motto —"praise in public, criticize in private"—he said, "Julie, Mark, Holly, we'll take a few minutes later this afternoon to go over what Mrs. Oliver wanted to talk with me about. In the meantime," he smiled, "onward and upward... Joon, who's our next patient?"

"Mrs. Lofton in room 522."

They turned down the hall and began the lengthy processes of seeing Ms. Lofton and the rest of their patients, changing diagnostic and treatment plans to address unrecognized findings and illnesses unearthed by talking with and examining each patient, as with Camilla. It took eight hours, interrupted by a brief lunch, before they were done.

Damen met with Julie, Mark, and Holly afterwards to discuss Mrs. Oliver's feedback. Gentle in relating what she said, he sought their perspectives about what had occurred, and without being judgmental, shared how they could have treated her better. The discussion seemed to be going well when Julie began sobbing, overcome by painful memories from growing up in a family destroyed by alcoholism.

Mark and Holly sat in silence, stunned, as Damen gave Julie a tissue. She composed herself and said, "I'm so sorry about Mrs. Oliver…" Taking a deep breath, she continued, "This has dredged up memories I can't share because they hurt so much. God knows I'll try to give the best care to my alcoholic patients, despite the misery and pain they cause loved ones." She cried in silence and tears poured down her cheeks.

Looking at Julie, to Mark, then Holly, Damen said, "Being a physician is hard—all of us have personal heartbreaks, disappointments, and shortcomings that affect our relationships with patients and how we treat them." His eyes showed understanding. "Think about this case, learn from it, and let's choose to be better people and physicians because of it." He hesitated. "We'll consider what we've discussed here as confidential, unless you three decide otherwise. I'll see you tomorrow morning." He stood up and left the room.

"Sorry..." Julie said to Mark and Holly, and they came over and gave her supportive hugs.

Then she added, "He *is* really good."

A short distance away, Damen was in a speed walk to his office—he had a lot to do before going home—and thinking about the day's events. *That last meeting with Julie, Holly, and Mark was a difficult one*, he reflected, *but overall, rounds went well and this team is a good one. The next few months should be a lot of fun.*

Then his phone rang. It was the University President with an unusual request.

CHAPTER 4 – A BENEFACTOR'S REQUEST

Penelope Liu, PhD, MD, watched from her office as groups of students meandered across the leafless, tree-lined academic quadrangle to winter classes. She had moved to Southern fourteen years ago after leading Palo Alto's renowned Pediatric Research Institute for a decade. As Southern's first female president, she was popular, fair, transparent, and had been able to satisfy the stakeholders of this historic institution: Board of Trustees, benefactors, faculty, students, parents, alumni, and others. This entailed responding promptly and thoughtfully to the needs and concerns of the school's wealthy patrons, people like Stuart Castelman.

A Southern University Board of Trustee member and CEO of America's largest life insurance company, Brantel Mutual, Castelman had called yesterday to discuss a confidential matter. Twenty-five years ago, Brantel wrote a twenty-million-dollar life insurance policy for a successful young businessman who later in life developed serious long-term medical problems. He was expected to survive beyond the policy's end date, but died without warning three months ago; his widow was the beneficiary.

Brantel's in-house consulting physician had reviewed the case and felt the man died from natural causes due to his chronic medical conditions. However, because of the policy's size and "additional circumstances," Castelman wanted the case investigated by another medical expert, someone able to think outside the box and comprehensively evaluate the death from a fresh perspective. Since Jack Damen had saved the life of his youngest son ten years ago, he considered him "the best damn physician in the world" and asked to buy some of his time.

Liu knew the son's story well because Castelman had called her that morning asking for help, and she was the one who made the calls needed for him to be seen at the hospital's Emergency Department "as soon as possible." By chance, Dr. Jack Damen had been working there.

Damen was about to leave Southern's ED after a

grueling Sunday night of rescuing sick patients when his Division Chief told him to see a VIP patient who had just arrived there. He said the son of a university Board of Trustees member had to be seen "right away by someone good."

Screw it, Damen thought, *I've been in the ED all night anyway*. He knocked and entered the exam room where a muscular young man sat in a chair.

"Good morning. I'm Dr. Damen." He shook the man's hand.

"The chart says you're Robert Castelman. You're twenty years old and a junior at the university. Is that correct?"

"Yes, sir. Please call me Bob. Only my parents call me 'Robert'."

Damen sat down on the swivel stool and said, "Bob, what brings you in today?"

"You're the third doctor in the last week, but my father's a worry-wart and thinks I need to be seen again—I was in a car wreck last Monday. I pulled out in front of another car and got hit on the driver's door. I felt OK, but they took me to the emergency room anyway and checked me out. Everything was fine and they sent me home.

"On Friday, my girlfriend took me to Hospital Urgent Care 'cause my side still hurt. They said it was 'muscles' and gave me some ibuprofen. It's still bothering me, so my dad called the university president to see what should be done. She said to come here, and he drove me over. He's out in the waiting room."

Damen gathered details about Bob's condition after the wreck and asked to examine him. Bob grimaced as he climbed onto the table.

After doing his exam, Damen said, "Bob, I'm concerned you may have injured your spleen and we're just now able to pick it up. I'm going to have our nurse start an intravenous line, an IV. This is a precaution while we get some additional tests. Also, I'm going to have your dad come back to the exam room so we can talk. Is that OK?"

"Sure."

Damen left the room and ordered an emergency abdominal CAT scan. When he returned, a tall man in his mid-fifties with salted brown hair and a well-tailored gray suit stood up from the bedside chair and extended his hand.

"I'm Stuart Castelman, Robert's father, and it's nice seeing you, Dr. Damen."

Damen said, "It's nice meeting you, Mr. Castelman. Thanks for coming back to the room. I've examined Bob, and I'm concerned about his spleen. Although the CAT scan of his abdomen after the wreck was negative, we sometimes see spleens rupture days after being injured. I've ordered a repeat CAT scan and had our nurse start an IV before we send Bob to Radiology for his test. Do you have any questions?"

Stuart asked, "Is a ruptured spleen serious?"

"Yes...because if the spleen breaks open, a lot of blood can be lost into the abdomen and it becomes a surgical emergency. That's why we started the IV —as a precaution. Any other questions?"

"No, not for now."

"Bob, how about you?"

"No."

Damen left the exam room, and the radiologist paged him within fifteen minutes. He reviewed the CAT scan with her and called the surgery team: the spleen was about to rupture and needed to be taken out. He explained this to the Castelmans.

Everything went smoothly until the third-year surgical resident examined Bob and said he was *not* going to take him to the operating room right away, that he had decided instead to monitor Bob's condition upstairs in a hospital room on the surgery floor. Damen talked with the resident in private, and as often happens when two sleep-deprived physicians disagree, the discussion degenerated into a pissing contest. Unable to convince the resident of the immediacy to remove the damaged spleen, Damen called the resident's supervisor, who expounded that delayed spleen injuries don't always rupture and that he agreed with the resident's plan.

Damen said, "Did you look at the CAT scan yourself or discuss it with the radiologist?"

There was no response.

He continued. "I did both, and that spleen is ready to rupture. Your resident seems really bright, but he got this one wrong. Before you decide not to take this kid to the OR, how about reviewing the CAT scan and examining the patient yourself? If that spleen blows on the floor and there's a bad outcome, the lawyers will have a field day. You'll see what I mean when you check things out yourself."

Thirty minutes later, after a large coffee, Damen called the ED and was told the patient had been taken to the OR. He learned later the spleen ruptured as soon as Bob's abdomen was opened. The surgery supervisor told the family afterwards that Damen "is an excellent doctor and likely saved Bob's life."

Liu had had mixed thoughts about asking Damen to be involved. *Castelman was a member of the Board of Trustees and a generous benefactor, but requests like his were often slippery slopes with one request*

leading to another. And if I had refused, I'd have to watch my back as long as he was on the Board. He's been an honest man but has held grudges when denied.

Whether Damen would agree to help was another matter. She suspected Thanksgiving and Christmas were not enjoyable for him—although his military PTSD seemed to be under control, most holidays since Beth divorced him had been psychological disasters filled with guilt-ridden flashbacks from their times together. However, he'd returned to work after the New Year's break and all appeared well: his teaching and patient care were as good as ever, and his research lab was humming along without any problems.

He might not want to risk messing things up, though, she thought. *He has been careful with commitments and will refuse if I don't make it worthwhile for him.*

Liu rescheduled an appointment so she could have quiet time to think. Then she made a few calls and contacted Damen.

CHAPTER 5 – THE ASSIGNMENT

What an interesting week, Damen thought as he sat in his study and looked at Jasper's large white teeth. The face mug, handmade in Seagrove, North Carolina, was filled with Costa Rican coffee from an expatriate anthropology professor who donates several bags whenever he returns to Southern for medical care. Its sweet, peppery smell helps Damen relax and think through complex issues, like the one facing him now.

He'd walked to Dr. Liu's office immediately after receiving her call and was nervous. They met every June for his annual evaluations, and every three to four months for other matters, but Januarys were busy and not the time for unimportant meetings. Her administrative assistant led him to an adjacent conference room where Liu waited.

Tall, book-lined shelves above polished dark-cherry cabinets framed a matching table and maroon leather chairs, and light from windows facing the quadrangle brightened the room, important for lifting spirits during Board of Trustees and other confidential meetings held there. This was the inner sanctum for power brokers at Southern University, where decisions of the greatest importance to the university's future were made, often after contentious debate. Damen had not known this room existed.

Liu turned from the window and, shaking his hand, said, "Jack, it's good seeing you again." She motioned to a seat across the table, and they sat down. "Did you have a nice Christmas and New Year's?"

He smiled and settled into the chair. "Yes, it *was* a good break. Emmi and I spent a lot of time together, and she hosted a huge family get-together where I met people from all ends of her family. They're good folks—I was invited to go quail hunting about five times—and it was super relaxing. All things considered, it couldn't have been better. How about you?"

"We had a good one also. I flew the family out to California so they could re-immerse in our culture." Laughing, she said, "Hearing our youngest speak Chinese with a North Carolina accent is painful. You should have seen the looks on the grandparents' faces."

Damen laughed and began to relax. He liked and respected Dr. Liu, and she him.

"Jack, I've asked you here today to make a proposal," and she recounted her discussion with Stuart Castelman.

Afterwards, she paused, eyes fixed on Damen, and continued with earnest. "I usually don't respond to Trustee requests like this, but Stuart has been a generous supporter of Southern for many years and a personal friend and ally of mine through some tough political situations—and I'd like to keep him that way.

"On the other hand, the last thing I'd want is for your involvement in this to precipitate another PTSD episode…one every year or two is plenty. I have mixed feelings talking about it, so if at any point you decide you're not interested, let me know and we'll forget this discussion ever took place." She hesitated. "Jack, you'll need to tell me if you feel this project will be too much."

Damen was silent. *Her relationship with Castelman must really be important for her*, he thought, *because this request is a lot to ask of a faculty member. I'm not worried about the PTSD, but with my Team 2 teaching responsibilities just starting, the timing couldn't be worse. And the benefits from this look all one-sided—hers.*

Liu shifted in her chair and continued with a faint

grin. "At this point, I have no doubt you're wondering, 'What's in it for me other than getting feel-good kudos from my boss?' Quite a bit, it turns out.

"Brantel Mutual will give Southern University a ten percent reward—their usual amount—if you determine the death wasn't from natural causes. That's two million dollars! If you agree to do this, I'll designate half to a medical student scholarship fund of your choice, or a research fund. I know you're contributing monthly to Beth's Fund; it's still small, and some or all of a million dollars would really give it a boost."

Damen said, "What if it turns out the guy died of natural causes?"

"Brantel will cover the cost of your faculty salary for as long as you're on the case, and I'll channel half of that into whatever fund you choose. It will be a lot less than the reward but still a good amount. I'll also arrange coverage of your night and weekend hospital responsibilities while you're working on this. That should free up the time you'll need."

Liu's smart, Damen thought, *and she's leveraging what matters most to me: students, research, and Beth. Of course Beth...*

He said, "This could do a lot for the student scholarship and research funds, like you mentioned." After a thoughtful pause, he added, "I should be able to manage it okay as long as the coverage you arrange works out and the investigation doesn't drag on too long. But before committing to anything, I'll need to think it through and meet with Castelman to learn the details of their client's death as well as Brantel's expectations of my role. I will let you know as soon as I've made a decision."

"That's great. Take your time—there's no rush—and call me as questions come up."

Damen left, and President Liu returned to the window, gazing out and wondering if she would regret asking him to be involved.

Later that night, Damen reviewed the pros and cons of accepting Liu's offer. He knew it would be a lot of work, but Brantel's medical consultants found nothing awry after they had examined the case; only Castelman's intuition was delaying settlement of the insurance claim. If he discovered the man did not die from natural causes—that he had been killed—the benefit to Beth's Scholarship Fund would be huge. On the other hand, if he determined the death had been natural, the Fund would still get a lot of money. That Liu was going to lighten his teaching responsibilities by taking away night and weekend call was key because it would reduce any psychological risk to him from exhaustion for taking this on.

The eight-hundred pound gorilla here, Damen mulled, *is how much this might affect my PTSD.*

Christmas was okay this year, but New Years was not great. If the investigation lasts too long or gets off track and too stressful, I dunno... I need to talk with Stuart Castelman.

They met for lunch at a small French bistro the next day. It was a local favorite, with delicious food, background music, and ample space between tables—perfect for a discreet discussion. Castelman's appearance was unchanged since Damen saw him a decade ago during Bob's hospitalization. Perhaps a few pounds heavier, but still the broad grin, firm handshake, and air of expected obedience characteristic of large company CEOs.

Reconnecting over soup and wine, Castleman recounted what had happened with Bob since that morning in the hospital. After he graduated from Southern, he moved to Phoenix and now headed up a Brantel Mutual office there. His two little boys, five and seven years old, were the apples of Grandpa's eyes. Damon, in turn, shared parts of his life, but didn't mention Beth or that she'd divorced him.

The rest of lunch and two hours afterwards were spent talking about Brantel's insurance case. The policyholder, Carlton Solishe, had died three months ago, and after reviewing the case, the company's in-house medical consultant determined it had been due to complications from chronic medical conditions. The size of the policy's death benefit was huge—the largest in the company's history—so Castelman, on a hunch, had delayed its payment and tasked Brantel's investigators with looking into Solishe's background to determine if he had had any enemies that might have wanted him dead. Their preliminary findings revealed he had been widely abhorred because of personal improprieties and were why Castelman asked President Liu for Damon's assistance in the investigation.

I don't get it, Damen thought, *what does he want from me, I mean, they've got their own doctor and investigators?* He said, "Stuart, your company's physician has looked into the death and found nothing suspicious about it. I'm a medical doctor, not a police detective, and your physician is good—I know his reputation—so what do you expect me to do that he's not already done?"

"Jack, you saved my son Bob's life after two physicians had missed the correct diagnosis and after the surgery resident failed to appreciate his spleen was about to rupture, not just because you had a lot of medical knowledge, but because you were able to perceive the entirety of the situation and its danger to him. Before asking Dr. Liu for your help, I had talked with several highly respected physician colleagues of yours at Southern and that's what you've become known for: having an uncanny ability to connect loosely associated dots into clinical pictures that others haven't recognized. That's what I want you to do for our investigation: review everything we've learned and are learning about Carlton Solishe, talk with his family and people they know, and connect the dots surrounding his death."

It sounds like a boatload of work and travel, Damen thought, *but he's paying a lot of money for it regardless of the outcome. I wonder what else he has to say.*

After Castelman shared additional details regarding Carlton Solishe's unexpected death, Damen said he'd look into it with the stipulation that Castelman guarantee him unfettered access to Soliche's medical records plus the insurance records. He also wanted full, ongoing disclosure with Brantel's investigative team working on the case. Castelman agreed and predicted the investigation would be closed within three months. Damen wasn't so sure.

He called President Liu later that afternoon with his decision and a forewarning that his involvement might last longer than anticipated: the circumstances surrounding the death that aroused Castelman's suspicions portended time-consuming medical rabbit holes that could lead anywhere.

The next day, he told Team 2 about Liu's request and his acceptance of her offer. Joon Kim and Julie McKenzie were pissed and didn't hide their anger. As upper-level residents, they'd have to work harder to teach, supervise, and maintain the team's quality of care. The others were disappointed, and emboldened by the upper residents, shared concerns about how their training might suffer.

Damen regretted they felt this way about his decision but reassured them at length about his commitment to their learning. Explaining this was something he needed to do, he also shared that all of this was new for him, and that he would do his best to not get distracted from his teaching responsibilities.

Looking at the junior residents and students, he said, "If you ever feel I'm letting you down as a teacher, please tell Joon or Julie. You can be honest with them—they'll let me know without identifying who's saying what. And they'll also be letting me know if I'm not doing my job. Joon knows he can say anything to me without fear of retribution, and you'll learn that too in due time. But for now, go through them." He hesitated, "Joon and Julie, is that okay with you?"

Joon looked at Julie, then back to Damen, and said stone-faced, "I suppose it will have to be. Don't worry, if things break down, we'll let you know—

that's for sure."

They talked some more, and as the surprise of Damen's announcement wore off, the team refocused on their patients and the day's business. Rounds got done, the teaching went well, and because the team wasn't on call, everyone went home at a good hour, the students and residents to get some needed sleep and Damen to think of next steps in his investigation.

"Where should I begin?" Damen whispered to Jasper and the study's walls. The voice of a physician mentor rang in his ears: "If you don't understand something, it means you need more information."

The comfortable leather chair, mellow jazz, and Jasper's potion softened the specter of the tasks that lay ahead.

CHAPTER 6 – FACES OF LOVE

The barren beds of pine straw around the building smelled fresh as they dried in the cool winter air. In a few months, they'd be alive with fragrant white, red, and pink roses, bees, and all sorts of crawling critters, but they were asleep for now. Inside, residents of Pineview Gardens Rest Home had settled into late-morning routines, some sleeping in their rooms or talking with friends, others strolling the halls, and regulars who sat in the reception area watching cars come and go through the circular driveway.

Medical Assistant Florence Mabry was walking through the halls and sitting areas and directing everyone to the dining room, where lunch would be served at noon. Getting folks to meals, recreational events, and other activities took a long time because of their physical or mental disabilities. The reception area was farthest from the dining room.

"Miss Beth, I thought I'd find you here. It's a beautiful day, but it's time for lunch. Isn't that great? We'll have some delicious food?"

The fortyish woman on the couch raised her vacant eyes and said in a strong monotone, "Already? I don't want to go."

It was the same every day.

"I know, but on the way you can pick up a chocolate for dessert and kiss Dr. Jack."

Her eyes widened and darted from side to side. "Okay," she said agreeably.

Beth's room was on the way to the dining room. It was warm and comfortable and decorated with plants, colorful wall art, and some family pictures. She went to the top of her dresser, carefully teased a foil-covered chocolate heart out of the box, and put it in her pocket. A picture of Jack Damen in his early thirties was next to the box. She stared at it for a moment, then took it in her hands and gave it a long, soft kiss.

Florence said as if addressing a child, "You used to be married to him. He visits every week and brings chocolates. You still love him, don't you?"

Beth smiled and said, "...Yes." Then she frowned with terror. "No."

"Miss Beth, let's go get some of your favorite hamburger steak, mashed potatoes, and corn."

Smiling again, Beth put the picture back on the dresser and held Florence's arm as they walked to the dining room.

As they ambled down the long hallway, Mabry recalled her discussions with Beth's mother, Kathy, and thought, *but for the grace of God go I*. They talked whenever it was convenient—she had visited Beth three times a week, on Mondays, Wednesdays, and Saturdays, until shortly before she died—and more often than not, the conversations returned to the same topics.

She spoke about how her husband had been a Marine and about the challenges of being a single parent and raising a small girl after he was killed in the Middle East. And how that sweet little girl missed her daddy, became withdrawn after he was gone, and seemed to find solace in playing a violin he had given her on the last Christmas they were together. Money was always a challenge, and the early teenage years became a painful gauntlet for Beth because of the cruelty from more prosperous and attractive classmates about her clothes, shyness, and gangly appearance. Then, traits from Kathy's mother took over.

Beth was a straight-A student, and during the junior and senior years of high school, her physical appearance caught up as she matured into a beautiful, dark-haired young woman with hazel eyes, the spitting image of her grandmother. And like Grandma, her talent for the violin blossomed.

The city's elite private university offered her a music and academic scholarship, but because the additional costs of attendance were prohibitive, she decided to live at home and attend the local community college, where she studied for an associate's degree in Library Science. Kathy considered this time with Beth to be a blessing because they became loving friends in addition to mother and daughter. After graduation, Beth moved into her own apartment and supported herself playing violin with the Rochester Philharmonic Orchestra and working as a part-time librarian at the medical school library. That's where she met Dr. Jack Damen and fell in love.

It was a whirlwind romance—Beth was happier than ever, and Jack worshipped the ground she walked on. A few years older than her, he had been in the military and like her father was a man's man, strong and tough, but he was a doctor and gentle and kind toward her. They got married in six months, moved south, and were happy until "something terrible happened to Beth in California," leaving her like she was now.

Kathy took her home in the hope she'd recover, but it never happened. Beth couldn't care for herself and it became clear she would be incapacitated for the rest of her life. Unmanageable at times—crying, screaming, and trying to leave the house—with Kathy's failing health, she had to be institutionalized and was placed here in Pineview Gardens. Kathy said it was the hardest decision she ever had to make.

The lunch tables were almost full by the time Beth reached her chair, shivering, moving slow, and searching in the crowd for faces from her past. *What happened in California must have been horrible*, Mabry thought as she looked on. *Kathy wouldn't talk about it, not a word, and she cried in her car after every visit with Beth—nobody said why she passed away, but I know a broken heart was a big part of it.*

CHAPTER 7 – DESPICABLE

The folders on the den table contained treasure troves of spicy information about Carlton Solishe and his family that were obtained by Brantel Mutual's investigative team through interviews, bribes, and coercion. Damen wanted to read about Carlton first, and with his coffee-filled face mug Jasper in hand, he was alternating between a file that contained his personal information and another with his medical history. Nothing had been left out.

People can be bought, Damen mused, and beyond the usual contacts for this type of investigation–the Solishes, their friends, neighbors, and professional acquaintances–Brantel's team talked with Carlton's prostitutes, illicit lovers, and others who just plain hated his guts. This approach, combined with analyses of bank and business records unknown to the IRS, allowed the team to retrace his life, and a shocking picture of an evil and perverted man emerged. All families have skeletons, but Carlton's behaviors had been so vile that Damen imagined Jasper's enameled eyes opening wider as secrets in the files were revealed.

Most degenerates contaminate their home fields first and Carlton was no exception. However, he was mega rich, and after his deviancy was unmasked in Chicago, he looked elsewhere to satisfy his appetites and discovered sexual bliss in Thailand.

Pathum Thani is a town north of Bangkok, where tourists go to escape the big-city bustle and tourist traps, pricey accommodations, and air pollution. It's also one of many sex trade centers in Thailand and the reason for Carlton's semi-monthly trips to the region. Frequent travel was expensive, but the pleasures he experienced there controlled his cravings back home.

Ecstasy was about to kill him, or so he thought. The full effects of the hashish cocktail hit Carlton as the young Thai girl stimulated him—his heart pounded, sweat stung his bloodshot eyes, and he wagged his face side to side within a hallucination of corpulent, hanging breasts. *If this isn't heaven*, he thought, *then I don't know what is. Last night with the boy was good, but this is great...* And he groaned with satisfaction as the girl heightened and prolonged his climax by using techniques of prostitutes well beyond her age. Sleep overcame him and he awoke the next day to the touches of another ten-year-old girl. This drug and sex binge, as others, would last three days.

Carlton was a closet bisexual pedophile and had managed to keep his illicit sexual preferences and practices hidden from his wife, Anita, until he raped the eight-year-old son of close family friends. Connections and a seven-million-dollar settlement kept him out of prison and the public's eye, but the judge made it clear that further episodes would land him behind bars for decades.

From Anita's friends, Brantel had learned she was devastated by news of the rape. After initial happiness in their marriage, she'd come to realize Carlton was a cruel man; however, she had not imagined he was that depraved. Divorce was tempting but escaping him would involve a brutal legal battle that could drag on for years, so she tried to rationalize what had happened despite her fears.

She asked the kids if Daddy ever touched them in their private areas, and after looking at each other, they cried uncontrollably while denying anything ever occurred. Her darkest suspicions grew when the children were sent to private boarding school the following semester; they seemed relieved to get away from him. She would never know if they'd been molested, but Carlton's moral turpitude was beyond doubt. And as a parent herself, she couldn't avoid thinking about his immigrant parents and the shame they would have suffered from this despicable affair.

Taras and Olesya Solodskikh had eked out a living in the Rostov district of the South Russia coal industry until they could no longer stand the miserable living conditions. They married, and with the encouragement of family and the prerequisite bribes to officials, they obtained visas and emigrated to Northeastern Pennsylvania in the United States. Coal mining was lucrative there and allowed them to live luxurious lives compared to Rostov. They shortened their family surname to Solishe, had three sons, and lived in the same home until their deaths.

The Solishe boys had been taken to affordable public clinics for medical care, and thanks to the State Health Department's microfilm files and Brantel's investigative team, Damen was able to review Carlton's childhood and adolescent medical records. Everything seemed routine: immunizations, occasional ear and throat infections, and mention of seeing a child psychologist for "headaches and stress." Clinic notes from teen school exams indicated good health, but there were a few red flags: "...now seeing psychiatrist," "...poor eye contact and odd affect," "...often lies to parents," "...aggressive with peers," "...seems disinterested in others," and "...not many friends."

Damen suspected Carlton was seeing the psychiatrist for a personality disorder, where friends and others know something's not right and don't like being around the person for an extended time. Severe cases can't function in society, but mild ones often go undiagnosed for years.

These were the first clues that something darker was growing within Carlton. As a physician, Damen understood you can't know what leads to a medical or life situation by looking only at what's in front of you. A person may have a heart attack today, but that occurs after years of preceding factors, such as advancing arteriosclerosis, high blood pressure, or diabetes. In a similar way, aspects like family support, education, ambition, and genetic predisposition play huge roles in a person's future career success. The determinants of Carlton's life-tale, Damen felt, had been rooted by the time he was an adolescent.

As Damen read, he learned that Carlton was the middle son and, to casual observers, lived an unremarkable childhood before college. A non-athlete, he was a member of his high school Chess Club and excelled academically. He was an introvert, had few friends, and not much of a social life.

A full scholarship to the flagship state university made his mother and father proud, and he received straight "A"s during his first year there. Shortly after the beginning of his sophomore year, his parents were killed in a motor vehicle accident by a drunk driver. Interviews with college acquaintances indicate Carlton did not talk about it afterwards or seem upset. He stopped seeing his psychiatrist and returned to his hometown only for occasional holiday visits with his brothers.

It was at university where his business acumen and unique personality traits blossomed. He graduated in three years, the only blemish on his transcript being an unprosecuted charge by a coed that he drugged and raped her. A Russian-backed venture capital firm hired him on the spot, and he worked there for ten years before starting Solishe Capital Inc. (SCI).

Carlton's gift for predicting business trends assured success for SCI in identifying and financing startup companies with disruptive technologies —for example, when companies producing computer-based word processing equipment displaced companies that manufactured typewriters. A timely, countrywide IT and manufacturing boom was a gold mine for the company, and within a few years, SCI became Chicago's top venture capital firm. Carlton was wealthy beyond his wildest dreams.

With wealth came civic responsibility, and altruism and philanthropy are hallmarks of the typical ultra-rich. Carlton, on the other hand, chose selfishness and detached arrogance as his legacies to the community. With no friends, and deviant sex as the only interest outside of work, his sociopathic tendencies surfaced in a consuming, new passion: destroying people's lives.

He took pleasure in engineering personal bankruptcies, getting people fired from their jobs, and closely following the tragic social consequences. Carlton confided without shame to a business partner how he became sexually aroused when his victims committed suicide, and that he enjoyed a forced, month-long sexual marathon with Anita after her father hung himself. His putrid Shangri-La didn't last long, though, before a debilitating stroke threw him into a permanent hellhole at age fifty-three.

Carlton was having sex with his two favorite prostitutes at the Summit Hotel when he suffered a heart attack after snorting cocaine. He grabbed his chest, lost consciousness, and they figured he was dead. After quickly removing his fantasy costume, the hookers called the front desk for 911. But he wasn't dead. When he opened his eyes and saw the face of the paramedic, he shouted, "What the hell is going on?" A slurpy "Uulahhh" was all that came out, and he realized he could not move his right arm and leg; also his left side was weak.

His heart attack had caused two strokes, one that paralyzed his right side and a smaller one that weakened his left arm and leg. They also affected his ability to communicate and swallow, and a feeding tube through his abdomen into his stomach was needed to prevent choking whenever he ate or drank. He seemed to understand his situation, and most of what was said to him, but became infuriated because he could not think of or speak words to express himself. He required 24/7 full-service nursing care, and until his death five years later, was confined to bed or strapped in a chair while he screamed unintelligibly at those around him.

Welcome to Hell, thought Damen, and not just for Carlton, but also for his wife and family who had to provide support and function as caregivers. Carlton's behaviors had been disgusting, but this was a nightmare nobody deserved: paralyzed on one side, dependent for feeding and personal hygiene, and unable to communicate except for gurgling, screaming, and flailing about with a weakened left arm and leg.

He continued to read.

The remaining records were from the copious medical services given to Carlton after his strokes: nurses, aides, and physicians who gave care at his home, clinic visits with medical specialists and skin ulcer teams, ambulance and EMT services, and emergency department visits and hospitalizations. The medical care was appropriate; Carlton's problems were typical for bed-bound paraplegics and nothing seemed out of the ordinary. Then he died.

Anita found him unresponsive in bed and called 911. Carlton stated before his heart attack and strokes that he wanted everything done to keep him alive, so he was transported to the local emergency department and underwent two hours of vigorous attempts at resuscitation before being declared dead. Anita didn't want an autopsy, but because his death was unanticipated, the case was referred to the coroner.

The autopsy failed to reveal a cause of death, so it was assumed he died of a heart arrhythmia or other undetectable cause. However, the report contained some unexplained findings—"unusual" skin changes—and Damen made a note to talk with the coroner about them.

Damen finished reading the files and tossed them across his desk. *Shit*, he thought, *if Anita's files are anything like these, I'm going to need something stronger than coffee.* So he poured a Scotch and took a break. The smoky Oban seeped into his tongue as he relaxed and thought about the hospital team.

Kim, McKenzie, and the others had settled down and adapted to his medical care philosophy and standards. Many patients had been discharged, including Mrs. Oliver whose diarrhea had stopped after her medications were adjusted, and the team had admitted a new batch of patients. Teaching was going well, paperwork was current, and patients were getting great care.

So with nothing else to distract him, he was back to the big question: why did Carlton Solishe die when he did?

Damen returned to the folders to learn about Anita.

CHAPTER 8 – ANITA

Opposites attract, so what's the opposite of shit? Damen wondered as he shifted his attention to Anita Solishe, Carlton's wife. Getting married was serious, and someone marrying Carlton would have to be naïve, duped, or decide the benefits outweigh any foreseeable negatives. So which was it for Anita, and what kind of person is she? Brantel Mutual dug down to bedrock gathering information and dirt on Carlton, and from the thickness of Anita's folder, it appeared they had done the same for her. Damen took another slug of Oban and opened the files.

Anita was born in Hungary to Istvan and Rebeka Kozma. As the eldest daughter, she spent her youth and early adolescence helping with household chores and raising her sisters and brothers. Fair skin and petite features belied uncommon physical strength and determination, and with psychological maturity and intelligence beyond her years, she served as a second mother for the family.

When Anita was fifteen, the family immigrated to the United States. Istvan was a machinist in Hungary and found a job in a Chicago tool and die company, where he worked long hours to support the family while Rebeka stayed home to raise the children. A thickset man, strong, with callused hands, he believed the father of a family was "lord of his castle." Whenever disagreements with family members couldn't be resolved with loud arguing, he resorted to physical intimidation and screaming. Istvan never struck Rebeka or the girls, but he used a belt on the boys when they were rebellious, with long-lasting effects: the girls grew submissive, the boys angry and fearful like beaten dogs. All felt this was normal family behavior.

Rebeka and Anita became good friends, less like mother and daughter, and they did housework and raised the family together. Their discussions were far ranging and, given Istvan's moods, often returned to the topic of aggression and other male characteristics. Anita heard many times, long before she had sex, that men's behaviors are based on three motives: to get in a woman's pants, to dominate other men, and to control their surroundings with violence or money.

This lesson liberated her. America was a country of limitless opportunities, she realized, where an attractive and smart woman could get whatever she wanted in life by using ingenuity and her physical attributes. After delivering the high school Valedictorian speech, her face was radiant as she looked forward to pharmacy school and a lucrative career helping people, especially successful men.

Anita met Carlton Solishe several years later when she was a retail pharmacist in Chicago. Early one evening, a black Mercedes-Maybach pulled up in front of the pharmacy and the driver came in with prescriptions for three medications: blood pressure and cholesterol lowering pills, and a narcotic for back pain. When asked for identification, he said he was picking up the prescriptions for his boss who was waiting in the car. After Anita told him she'd need to give the narcotic tablets directly to the patient, Solishe came into the store, was condescending and belligerent, and made it clear he didn't like being there. However, he enjoyed talking to the attractive blonde pharmacist who was articulate and intelligent, chuckled at his sarcasm, and exuded sexuality.

Anita knew a gold mine when she saw one, and after a tactful refusal to dinner that evening, she accepted subsequent offers and became well known to his circle of venture capitalists. Solishe seemed to be a typical alpha male—aggressive and focused on money, power, and sex. Since Anita had similar interests and even stronger libido, the relationship flourished and they were married after a raw, passionate, and sex filled courtship. Solishe's business mushroomed, he bought the North Shore estate, and Anita was living her dream.

The estate was impressive, even by North Shore standards, and Anita was given full rein to furnish and fix it up. Money was no object, and with the help of landscapers and interior decorators, she transformed it into the envy of the community. New friends surfaced and Carlton and she were drawn into the social whirlwind of the neighborhood's "rich and famous."

People didn't like Carlton, nothing new there, but they enjoyed Anita's buoyant and kind personality. She seemed genuine, was interested in people's lives, and showed acts of friendship uncommon in their social strata: walking neglected newspapers to porches, returning stray dogs, calling and sending cards on birthdays, and cooking family dishes when folks were ill. She was invited to join a local book club, and because she was discreet and tight-lipped, became a trusted confidant to spouses of local elites who introduced her to the concepts of community service and philanthropy.

This had led to volunteering at the nearby Chicago Botanic Garden, where she continued to exercise her green thumb; neighbors often joked, "Anita can grow flowers on concrete." The Botanic Garden was a great place to meet fellow floriculturists and make new friends, and with the support of her social connections, she was chosen to serve on its Board of Directors as a Vice Chair.

She also had supported the Holocaust Museum and Education Center in Skokie, where she volunteered with others to ensure WWII's darkest scar wasn't forgotten. The Center welcomed her with open and sympathetic arms after she described the massacres of non-Jews in Rebeka's clan during the Hungarian Holocaust. Serving there provided a refreshing respite from the North Shore's social scene, where wealth often seemed more important than kinship and heritage, the lynchpins to Anita's self-esteem. Weekend trips into the city to be with siblings and their families provided additional relief and nourishment for her uncommon affinity with family roots.

Her parents, Istvan and Rebeka, had remained in their Chicago home after the children grew up and left. Anita and her sisters, Julia and Rahel, settled nearby while her brothers, driven away by Istvan's abuse, scattered across the Midwest. Every week after church, the parents had hosted the three sisters' families for Sunday dinner—Carlton was a nonbeliever and never attended—and after their deaths, the tradition was continued at Rahel's and Julia's homes. With the love and support of family, renewed each week at these gatherings, Anita stayed anchored as she raised her young son and worked to repay America for such a full and happy life. Carlton, who never felt close to his parents or siblings, couldn't understand the importance of the gatherings for Anita but nonetheless was supportive. At first.

Things began to change after the birth of their second child, a little girl. A workaholic and loner, without friends or outside interests, Carlton never had anything good to say about anyone. This worsened as he became richer, when everyone became "a stupid bastard," "low class," "uglier than a dog's ass," "a dumb shit," and so on. He became critical of Anita and stopped saying anything nice about her except she was "really good in bed." She excused herself whenever Carlton, after a few drinks, shared with acquaintances graphic specifics regarding where and how she made him feel good. Fracture lines in the marriage, narrow and stable until then, widened into crevasses.

Their relationship had been sustained by sex, but this was before his personality darkened, his pedophilia was exposed, and he began traveling to Thailand for kicks. She felt his behavior was disgusting, and they didn't have sex except when she was too drunk to fight him off; frustrated, Carlton would overpower and rape her despite her garbled pleas. When that began to lose its thrill for him, he tried to control her finances.

Anita wrote all the checks related to household matters, paid bills on time, was organized, and kept their home well stocked and clean. Her home phone rang throughout the day as she dealt with local businesses and friends called to get advice or just talk. When Carlton got home late, the phone would still be ringing.

It really pissed him off—he had no close friends and rarely got a home phone call. His anger grew and he began sharing his frustrations with his office assistant and other associates at SCI. *Everyone's calling her and all she does is sit on her ass around the house doing nothing. She's good looking and gets along with everyone, but people don't call because of that—it must be for money. She's spreading it around, and that's what the fucking blood suckers want; they're just playing her for a fool. I'll straighten that out… She's not going to hand out any more of my money.*

When he told her he would be taking over the household finances, Anita's response was immediate: eyes wide and locked on his, face drawn and pale, hands shaking, she screamed, "You can kiss my ass when I walk out that door with the kids." He was flabbergasted. Not many people told Carlton Solishe to kiss their ass, but Anita did and she meant it.

She had come to realize he was a heartless bully, and she was not about to let him ruin her life. If he put *any* restrictions on her household budget, the money that allowed her independence, she would divorce him and get as much of his fortune as possible. She wouldn't have the lifestyle she had now, but she'd do just fine.

Picturing the loss of millions, Carlton gathered himself and said, "I didn't realize this would be such a hot button issue." He thought how good it would feel to punch her in the face but held his arms back. "Let's just keep everything the way it's been. I've had a couple of hard weeks at work and need to chill out a bit."

The moment passed as their emotions cooled, but it lay bare the unsteady, three-legged foundation of their relationship: money, image, and sex.

She's a real bitch, Carlton thought afterwards as his twisted mind engineered their worsening relationship into a wicked game with winners and losers. *It'll cost me a shitload of money if she wants a divorce and calls one of her Jew lawyer friends, but hell, I'll treat her like a fucking queen and she won't even know when I stick it to her*. He sneered and picked up the phone.

Damen's hands were shaking as he closed the file and thought about his ill-fated marriage to Beth.

Anita had stayed married despite the evil in Carlton Solishe's heart, while Beth had divorced Damen after seeing the evil in his—an inclination to kill without regret—in California.

CHAPTER 9 – HELL BY THE BAY

Damen thought about Beth every day, every damn day, and reading about Carlton and Anita Solishe started his emotions roiling again. When they spilled out of control, when heartache coiled around his stomach and he bawled like a baby, that's when he went to the river and Emmi to be healed. *It isn't bad now,* he told himself, but his self-destructive avatar was growing again: *"Beth divorced me because I was a selfish bastard and never told her about South America and my dark side. If I had, she wouldn't have married me, and her life wouldn't have been wrecked in San Francisco. It would have been better if I died twenty-five years ago in the drug wars."*

Columbia and San Francisco seemed like yesterday.

◆ ◆ ◆

"Look at the flat-headed bastards," said Sargent Sam Tasker as he drove Army Ranger Corporal Jack "Claws" Damen on a dirt road through a small city in the Cauca region of Columbia. "They may be small, but they're mean as hell, and they'll slit your throat to keep the coke flowing to the U.S. It's their livelihood and they protect it, let me tell you."

It was Damen's first day in Columbia as part of covert U.S. Army operations against the drug cartels, and Tasker was his driver and guide—something he did for all newcomers to his squad. A bald, dark skinned, Pittsburgh native from the inner city, the sargent's thick neck and arms broadcast, "Don't mess with this man."

He had been in Columbia for three years as part of efforts by the U.S. Army's Special Operation Forces to counter the swelling cocaine flood entering the United States. The Ranger unit here was responsible for arresting wanted criminals and rescuing hostages; it was dangerous and deadly work: ten soldiers had been killed in the last year, two from Tasker's squad. Without exception, they had been captured in close combat encounters, then tortured and mutilated to discourage others from future interference. The Army's response was straightforward: bring in hand-selected enforcers, people like Damen, with the skills and mindsets to exact revenge and kill without remorse.

The unit's Commanding Officer in Cauca, Lieutenant Reyes, had briefed Tasker yesterday on his new squad member. "Sam, your new corporal—Damen's his name—should help keep the locals away from the rest of the squad. His nickname is 'Claws,' and if they try him out, they won't do it again. I talked with battalion headquarters at Fort Benning and they said he has the fastest and strongest hands they've ever seen and an aggressive attitude to match. And he never complains: he does what you order him to and doesn't say a word...quiet and tough as hell, they said."

Quiet? That's an understatement, thought Tasker, as he pointed out members of the local cartel loitering outside the dusty, broken-down storefronts. *The kid hasn't said ten words since I met him... I hope he's a good listener because whether he lives or dies will depend on how much of what I'm telling him sinks in.*

The sargent didn't know about Damen's near-total recall and that he could repeat every syllable of the most prophetic and important survival lesson taught to him that day: don't judge the people around here by their words or how they dress... check out their eyes; that is where the truth lies. Over the next two years, "Claws" looked into the telltale eyes of many cartel killers as the unnatural hand speed and strength that begot his nickname left a deadly trail—not only of bodies but also across his soul.

Damen decided to leave the Rangers following a bloody small arms and knife fight where he killed four cartel henchmen in a hotel room when they came looking for an informant. One had been a fifteen-year-old girl and he slit her throat without a second thought. But afterwards her youth and size reminded him of classmates he had dated in junior high school, and over the following weeks, the sliver of his conscience that remained after all the lives he'd taken in Columbia screamed, *Why did you have to kill her? What have you become?* Looking at himself in the mirror, he recognized the eyes of a cold-blooded killer, and his resolve to continue as an executioner for his country buckled. It was time to quit.

His separation from the military and return to civilian life was delayed and dragged on for months because he appeared indifferent about having killed so many people: the army wasn't about to release a merciless killer into society. But with counseling, it became obvious his demeanor hid self-loathing, a bloodguilt that could be treated. The protective mental walls fell with psychotherapy and he was able to confront his dark side—that he enjoyed killing "bad" people—and the realization his inner conflicts with making moral choices during situations involving good versus evil would be life-long. As important, his psychiatrist, Doctor Josiah King, encouraged him to pursue a career healing people instead of harming them.

"Jack, this is our last session before you leave the service. Have you thought about what you're going to do when you return home?"

"No, not really. Get a job, I guess. Somewhere in Upstate New York but not in Camillus—Mom's still alive and my sister lives nearby, but there isn't much work around there anymore. Maybe I'll see what's available in Syracuse."

"You told me your father died when you were in junior high?"

Damen said, "Yeah, his emphysema finally got him…smoking and the years grinding blades in the knife factory, you know."

"You got good grades in high school and set all sorts of records playing lacrosse, so why didn't you go to Syracuse or another university on a sports scholarship? I mean, they offered them to you, right?"

"Sure, but I wasn't ready for it…and we didn't have the money. There were lots of things the scholarships didn't pay for, and we were dirt poor. Mom worked two jobs so we'd have clothes like the other kids. Hell, half of my lacrosse equipment was secondhand from friends in town or the Onondaga Reservation."

"So you joined the Army and, as they say, the rest is history."

Damen took a deep breath and lowered his eyes. "I guess so."

"Jack, you need to see if you can get a lacrosse or veterans scholarship to go to college. If not, you'll need to find other ways to pay for it. You have too many gifts—you're smart, tenacious, have unbelievable hand-eye coordination, and under that tough-as-nails shell is a good person—you could help a lot of people. I think you should go to college and, if you do well there, go on to medical school and become a doctor. It might not work out, but you should aim for that."

Damen was stunned. After the months of psychotherapy, Dr. King knew him better than anyone, and here he was, telling him he had the ability to become a doctor and make the world a better place. No one, not a soul, had shown that level of confidence in him. Sure, they said he could get into college on a lacrosse scholarship, but nothing about getting somewhere with his mind or helping others.

King continued, "If you decide to go to college, let me know and I'll write a letter of recommendation for you."

Damen didn't know what to say. His parents were the only people who ever tried to help him like this, but he was a kid and too much of a damned fool to listen to them. *The last couple of months of therapy with Dr. King have been tough,* he thought, *but he's always been straight up with me. It would be hard, but maybe he's right and I'll be able to do it.*

Stripped of illusions about what he'd done in the Rangers and aware he'd carry its burden forever, Damen followed Dr. King's advice and decided to devote the remainder of his life to healing people instead of harming them. A lacrosse scholarship, supplemented with veteran benefits, allowed him to attend college. He did well in the prerequisite university courses and testing, and received a needs-based scholarship to attend Johns Hopkins Medical School, where he continued to excel. The Family Medicine residency in Rochester, New York, followed.

That's where he met Beth, a part-time librarian at the hospital library, and was smitten the first time they talked. She was the yin to his yang—shy, sensitive, and gentle, a professional violinist whose world was infused with music and kindness toward others.

He learned she was an only child and that she was close to her mother and elderly aunt, her only living relatives. The love and tenderness they shared appealed to Damen—there was none of this in his family—and he envisioned a life with Beth where they would have a family and children surrounded by love, an oasis of happiness and peace that he could protect from the harshness and dangers of life.

Beth too fell in love, having found a man that she felt comfortable with and could trust. Like her father, Damen had served in the military and was strong with a kind and humble face etched by the strains of war. And like her dad, he wouldn't talk about his experiences in the service except to express gratitude to God every Sunday in church that those days were behind him. When she questioned him about them, he would say, "There are some things I can't talk about...," and she'd let it go, feeling in her heart what Dr. King had discovered, that at core he was a good man.

They married just before his residency and fellowship at Hopkins. Afterwards, the job at Southern opened up and they moved to North Carolina.

It was Beth's first extended time away from Rochester, away from her mother and aunt, the Symphony Orchestra, the library, her friends and co-workers, and she struggled with severe loneliness. Damen's long hours as a resident in the hospital made this worse, but he recognized what she was going through and went home to be with her whenever possible. With his encouragement and tender support, she reached out into the City of Medicine music community, to people with interests and likings similar to hers.

The local City Orchestra was nowhere near as sophisticated as the Rochester Philharmonic Orchestra, and Beth was accepted into its ranks with open arms. New friends and acquaintances followed, her loneliness dissipated, and she began to embrace the slower pace and geniality of southern culture.

Damen completed his Internal Medicine Residency and Endocrinology Fellowship, and he was hired as a faculty member by Southern University School of Medicine. Each position allowed him more time to be with Beth and they cherished being together; their love matured and playful discussions about having children became more frequent. With his good-paying job, they bought a small house on the Pamlico River, where it widens behind the Outer Banks, and after a busy week at work, they'd relax in their deck chairs with their favorite beverages—Scotch for Damen and lemonade for Beth—and talk for hours as they watched boats go by. Happy days and weeks passed, and the future looked bright.

Then they traveled to San Francisco for Damen to do research, and their lives were destroyed.

Two years into his faculty position at Southern, Damen was offered a four-month position at San

Francisco Medical Center to do collaborative research on thyroid cancer. It was a dream come true: he could do research with international experts, and Beth could have some well-earned R&R from teaching music at Primrose Charter School. Long overdue for a romantic getaway, they couldn't wait to work and play in one of the most beautiful cities in the world.

Beth was more excited than Damen: she'd only flown twice before and hadn't traveled west beyond the Mississippi River. She kept saying—prophetic in retrospect—"I can't believe it...it's the trip of a lifetime."

They flew out in September, a magical time in San Francisco when visitors can explore its neighborhoods and hills under warm blue skies and experience a kaleidoscope of businesses, cultures, and lifestyles unparalleled in North America. The medical center had nearby rental homes and Damen and Beth found a nice one: two stories and a basement, on a quiet street, a few feet of grass in front and back, and a wonderful back porch for potted plants and fresh herbs and space for Beth to roll out her yoga mat.

The neighborhood had a few run-down houses but seemed safe and was within easy walking distance of Damen's lab. They quickly settled into the routine of Damen leaving for work at 7:30 each morning and returning at around 4:30 in the afternoon.

Beth would do housework and practice yoga in the mornings, read on the porch or do some gardening afterwards, and explore the city in the early afternoons. Dinners were casual and often with new friends, wine was plentiful, and they were enjoying every minute of being together. Until September fourteenth.

Damen left the laboratory early that day and thought he'd surprise Beth by greeting her when she returned to the house after her walk. He didn't know that she had arrived home two hours earlier. It was a beautiful day on their street: the sun was out, the warm breeze was cool on his face, and bright green leaves fluttered in the scattered trees. Damen noticed the old car with faded paint and dirty wheels in front of the house next door as he walked up the front steps. *What the hell?* he thought, seeing the splintered door jamb around the latch of the closed door. *Beth!*

He opened the door and heard subdued female cries and male voices upstairs. His gut raged, and he raced to get his .45 out of its secret place in the den. In a heartbeat, he was back in Cauca, Columbia, and "Claws" Damen and death crept up the carpeted stairs. Blood speckled the floor outside the cracked door that muted Beth's groans.

Damen entered the large bedroom without a sound. Beth had been pummeled into submission; her face was bloodied and deformed, and her torn clothes were scattered on the floor. The three hoods had raped her for over an hour, one after the other, and had thrown her from the bed onto the floor afterward to complete their assault; now finished, they were about to shoot her and make their getaway.

Sensing another presence, the punk standing over her with the handgun turned his head toward the door as a 230-grain jacketed hollow point bullet entered his forehead and blew his brains onto the wall behind him. The other two hoods were unarmed and instinctively raised their arms in surrender before they met the same fate. It was over in less than four seconds.

Beth, barely conscious, witnessed it all and now whimpered naked in fetal position beneath the three-eyed corpse; a broken broom handle rested on the floor beside her. Damen threw the body off, gently covered her with a blanket, and checked her pulse as she struggled against his touch. He left the room to quickly search the house and kill anyone else that was there; it was empty.

Returning upstairs to where Beth remained curled under the blanket, he found her gibbering and staring straight ahead. She wouldn't acknowledge his presence except to whimper and pull away when he touched her; however, she seemed physically stable and there was no bleeding from between her legs.

His stoic mindset crumbled as he began to piece together the enormity of all had been done to Beth. *God, no...no,* he thought, *Why? Why to her?* Emotions were about to overwhelm him when his medical background shouted, *An ambulance and the police need to be called ASAP.* And there was another problem, a big one.

Damen knew he'd be arrested and put in jail: he'd just killed three people, only one had a gun, and it was illegal for citizens of San Francisco to be armed except in special circumstances. That he brought his handgun into California and the city without permission would be an additional crime. Prison seemed certain, and he'd be away from Beth and never allowed to practice medicine again.

He started to shake. *Beth, poor Beth*, he thought, and tears poured down his face as Cauca, Columbia, faded away and the totality of what just happened gripped him. He needed help, in many ways, and remembered a lifeline he thought he'd never use. It was time to call in a favor.

It had been eight years since Damen talked with the elder Sicilian outside the Rochester Hospital Intensive Care Unit. The ICU was the final rotation in his Family Medicine Residency before he returned to Hopkins, and it allowed Damen to treat the sickest of the sick. He was in his wheelhouse there, and the other doctors recognized it. Talking with the Sicilian that morning, Damen's faculty supervisor credited Damen with saving the life of the wayward son who injected crushed diet pills into his veins to get a high.

Damen's after-shift work over four long nights while the old man watched and prayed made the difference. The Sicilian was still mourning the death of a daughter who had been murdered in Buffalo fifteen years before, and losing his remaining child would have killed him. Later that day, over espresso, Damen was given a phone number and told to call if he ever needed anything, *anything at all.*

"Yeah," said the accented female voice

"Hello, I'm Dr. Jack Damen and I need to talk with Mr. Cirazzi."

"He can't come to the phone right now."

"Would you please tell him Dr. Jack Damen, who he knows from the Rochester Hospital eight years ago, needs to talk with him as soon as possible. It's an emergency. Please ask him to call me back at this number."

"I'll give him the message."

Damen's phone rang within three minutes. "Dr. Damen, Jack, I didn't think we'd ever talk again. Donny's doing well these days, off drugs and helping in the family businesses, all thanks to you. What's going on?"

Damen quickly explained everything and that he didn't know if Cirazzi could help him from so far away.

"Doc, I've got family out there. So what's your address?" Damen gave it to him. "Stay where you are and don't call the ambulance or police yet. There should be someone knocking on your door within 30 minutes. You just do what they say, then you can call the police and ambulance, and whoever else you need to. For now, don't call anyone, OK?"

"Got it," Damen said, and hung up. He had been apprehensive about calling Cirazzi, but he thought, *It's been done now… All I can do is wait and hope for the best.*

He went back upstairs to the bedroom and stepped over the bodies to Beth, still curled on the floor under the blanket; she was babbling in a high pitch. He sat down and tried to reassure her, but she shrieked at his touch and drew her knees up in panic. Damen's eyes welled up and he sobbed uncontrollably at the damage done to his gentle flower.

The knocks on the front door came twenty-five minutes after Damen hung up the phone. The guys on the other side were dressed as air conditioning repairmen.

"Dr. Damen, I'm Dave and this is Tom. Mr. Cirazzi told our employer you have a problem."

Damen led them into the den and explained what had happened. He told them about Beth's condition and that she needed medical help as soon as possible.

Dave said, "Doc, don't ask how, but we know about your Ranger years and what you did in Columbia. This type of thing isn't new to you and we're assuming what you're telling us is spot on, but you're looking a bit shaky. Are you thinking clearly, or do we need to sit down and take a short break?"

He took a deep breath and said, "No, I'm all right for now." *This better be short, though,* he thought, *because my self-control is about gone…"*

"Good. Are you sure there was only one gun?"

Damen said, "Yes. He was pointing it at Beth when he saw me."

"Did the other two have any weapons when you offed them?"

"Not that I know of."

Tom said, "OK. When we go upstairs, will your wife know we're there?"

"I don't know, she's talking like a baby and looking away from the mess. I've got a blanket over her and I'll try to shield you from her view. Just don't say anything or she may start screaming again."

Dave said, "I understand. Doc, we'll need three to four minutes to do our thing and then we're going to come downstairs here to have a talk to wrap things up. Any questions before we go upstairs?"

"No." Damen just hoped they would be quick. Beth was in bad shape, and after what she'd been through, knowing more strange men are in the room could make her a lot worse.

He led them into the bedroom where Beth faced away from the carnage making unintelligible noises under the blanket; she seemed unaware of their presence. Damen stepped over the bodies, sat down on the floor behind her, and used his military training to keep his emotions in check. He wouldn't be able to last much longer. Dave and Tom worked fast and he followed them downstairs to the den.

Dave said, "Doc, listen to me carefully. All of those guys had guns—they're there now—and they reached for them when they saw you. Got it? Don't touch a thing upstairs until after the medics and police get here. Now, you have some problems: your gun is illegal in this city, and not many people can do head shots when they see their wife in such distress. So it's going to come out that you were in the Rangers, but don't say anything about it now.

"Your story is simple: You came home early and found the front door busted in. Beth was upstairs screaming. You've been in the Army and brought a pistol with you when you drove out here for your research month, so you took it upstairs. Those guys were raping her and reached for their guns when they saw you. You were convinced that they were going to kill you, so you shot them. Act in shock and don't say anything more until your lawyer, T.G. Fitzpatrick, gets here."

Dave continued. "That reminds me, give me your phone." He took it in a gloved hand and went upstairs to take some pictures. He returned, dialed a number, and handed the phone to Damen. "This will be Mr. Fitzpatrick. Act like you know him and say you've had a home invasion and you shot the intruders, that's all."

Damen took the phone as it was answered by a male voice. "Mr. Fitzpatrick, this is Jack Damen and I need your help. Some guys broke into my house and I shot them."

"Jack, I'll be right over." The line went dead.

"Who is this Fitzpatrick guy? I don't have a lawyer."

Dave said, "Yes you do, and he'll save your ass. Be sure to tell him you took some pictures with your phone—The cops will try to screw you because you had a gun, but the pictures will let Fitzpatrick set things straight. Doc, we're leaving, so as soon as we drive away you call the police and ambulance. Be sure to stick to the story until Fitzpatrick gets here. By the way, that was some sweet shooting."

Damen watched them drive away and called 911 and the police before walking upstairs to be with Beth. She was still under the blanket whimpering and crying and didn't respond to him at all except to jerk away from his touch. Damen's tough heart broke and he started to sob as the police, medics, Fitzpatrick, and onlookers flooded his house and existence; tears rolled down his face as the viciousness of what had happened hit him. And this was just the beginning.

The following weeks were a jumble of emotions, medical decisions, judicial wrangles, and soul searching for Damen. Damage to Beth's pelvic organs and rectum had been severe and required two separate surgeries and removal of her uterus. Every day, Damen worried about her condition—and tried hard not to interfere with her treatment—but she was in good hands.

The best abdominal trauma surgeon and psychiatrist had appeared in the Emergency Department when the ambulance arrived, courtesy of the long reach of Cirazzi, and the care she received was top notch. Damen and Beth were treated as VIPs throughout the hospitalization, prompting many to wonder, "Who do they know?"

Beth's mother flew out to visit and cried with Damen when she saw the curled up and fearful person her beloved daughter had become. Friends called, and after hearing the sadness and fatigue in Damen's voice, kept calling to give him support. That, and the help he received in navigating the city's legal minefields, kept him psychologically afloat during the immediate aftermath.

In San Francisco, like other big cities, judicial outcomes are often determined by politics, socioeconomic status, and personal contacts. And firearms are frowned upon there, especially when their illegal use leaves dead bodies within the city limits. Fortunately, Cirazzi hired T.G. Fitzpatrick, the legendary attorney of the rich, famous, and crooked in San Francisco, to represent Damen.

Fitzpatrick was known throughout the city for his successful defenses of Mob members, his leonine white hair, tan complexion, and perfect smiling teeth at center stage with clients in the celebratory post trial photo-ops. He was brilliant in the courtroom, and outside, and often avoided legal charges against his clients by knowing the misdeeds of every judge in the city.

He knew the exact amount Opero Construction had deposited in Judge Artero Ramirez's offshore account following the judge's dismissal of corruption charges against the company, and he let the judge know it in a private meeting while Damen's case was being reviewed. This, the work by Dave and Tom at the house, the photographs, and the grizzly nature of the assault on Beth ensured no charges would be brought against Damen. Even his pistol was returned to him under the pretense the dead rapists might have vengeful friends.

Fitzpatrick shook Damen's hand afterward and said, "Mr. Cirazzi will cover any additional legal help that might be needed. Just give me a call."

Beth was placed in the hospital Psychiatric Ward following her surgeries and remained there for three weeks. Damen visited daily and sat in the corner while she rocked and curled in bed looking away from him. Female nurses and aides cared for her because the sound of male voices, including Damen's, caused flashbacks of the assault; her screams of terror echoed through the ward.

The psychiatrist caring for Beth specialized in rape survivors and told Damen this was the worst case she'd seen. She also saw he was struggling and agreed to see him as an outpatient in her office. It saved his life.

Damen's guilt for accepting a research position "in this wretched city" was overwhelming. And, the return of hellfire in his soul, the willingness to kill without conscience, pulled him further under. His delusion that it would remain dormant and Beth would never know that side of him evaporated when he killed the rapists without mercy as she watched.

Memories of Columbia howled, and Damen felt empathy for the spouses of the ruthless bastards and killers he'd sent to the grave. *I'm a murderous son-of-a-bitch too*, he thought, *and now it's Beth who will be scarred forever. If I had been at home that day instead of her, I could have died in the struggle—it would be better if I weren't alive.*

The psychiatrist was good, and she had help from Cirazzi's people who obtained copies of Damen's classified military files. She learned about the drug war and how killing was a big part of his job. And that he had walked away and since devoted himself to healing and preserving life. Meeting Beth, coupled with a newfound religious faith, had led him to believe that forgiveness and mercy for his military wrongdoings was possible. Beth's injuries from the attack had shattered that belief.

She met with Damen daily to help him move beyond suicidal thoughts and discover renewed purpose in life; she'd done this for rape victims and their families for years, but with less frequent appointments. Expensive even by San Francisco standards, her fees were paid by Cirazzi, who told her he would pay for however many sessions were needed.

Damen started to respond and regain his faith during the second week of therapy and was expected to fully recover. Beth's prognosis was far different: while allowing hope for a normal future, the psychiatrist was honest with Damen about how Beth had been affected by the rape and seeing him, a husband she'd always known as kind and gentle, execute her attackers. Hearing only the positive and blinded by his wishful vision of returning home and being able to rebuild their previous lives without long-lasting scars in their relationship, Damen didn't pick up the warning that Beth might never allow herself to be touched by him or any man.

Psychiatric care was arranged for Beth at a hospital in Raleigh, North Carolina, and she was flown there by medical transport. Her mother moved down from Rochester; Beth was discharged home with her after three weeks in the hospital. They lived near Southern, and Damen visited several times each week hoping for a recovery that never came.

It took four months before Beth could look at Damen without screaming and, haunted by memories, she filed for divorce the following year. Unable to hold down a job because of flashbacks and paranoid behavior, she stayed with her mother who had health problems of her own. Beth's mental health deteriorated and, without financial resources, she faced placement in a state psychiatric hospital. With her mother's blessing, Damen intervened and Beth was placed in a high-end nursing home located within thirty minutes of Raleigh and Southern Medical Center.

Pineview Gardens nursing home was beautiful but not affordable for most, even physicians. Damen started working Emergency Department shifts at Southern to make extra money so he wouldn't have to sell the river home—being near friends and his relationship with Emmi anchored him. Then one day, the nursing home administrator called saying a check for half of the month's expenses arrived from an attorney in Rochester; an accompanying letter stated a check would be coming every month.

Damen pulled out his cell phone and made a call.

"Yeah," said the familiar female voice

"Hello, this is Doctor Jack Damen and—"

She interrupted him. "He can't come to the phone but said you might be calling. He told me to tell you, 'That's what friends are for.' Anything else?"

"No, I just wanted to thank him."

"I'll tell him." And she hung up.

Damen looked at the phone with mixed emotions. He would be able to pay the balance of Beth's bills at Pineview Gardens from his regular salary without having to moonlight, but after this and Cirazzi's help in San Francisco, he'd be indebted to him forever. *Maybe I can find a way to pay him back...that would be the best situation...or maybe he'll ask for something in return.*

He sighed in resignation. *In any case, Beth will be able to stay there and her care will be top notch. And while she may not love me anymore*—he pictured her face during the good days at the river and closed his eyes—*she sure enjoys those chocolate hearts I leave on her dresser every week.*

CHAPTER 10 – COFFEE AT THE NORTH SHORE

The Solishe estate was nestled in an exclusive neighborhood on the North Shore, where the super-rich lived in luxury behind landscaped stands of trees, bushes, and tall native grasses. A tasteful wrought iron "S" marked its private drive that wound from the county road past a hidden guardhouse, through thick woods, and into a circular parking area in front of the Neo-Georgian mansion. Ceramic vessels filled with seasonal flowers framed the columned porch, and a narrow gravel road continued behind the home to the stocked lake, stables, and large English garden.

Anita Solishe and Carlton's longtime attorney, Gene Rusco, sat in the informal dining room at the back of the house, where Anita's foul mood contrasted with the morning sun that beamed through the large windows. Rusco had informed her yesterday that Brantel Mutual intended to investigate Carlton's death further before paying out the life insurance benefit. He told her this was not unusual with large policies, but she didn't seem to hear him.

She said, "Did they give any reasons for this?"

"No, just that this procedure is routine when deaths with large policies happen."

"I thought a team had already worked on it and they were ready to wrap things up."

Rusco said, "I thought so too, but they want some hot-shot doctor from Southern Medical Center to take a look and make sure he died of natural causes."

"What the hell are they thinking? That I killed him? Or someone else killed him? His Will left me in good shape and I don't need the twenty million dollars, so as far as I'm concerned, this is a bunch of crap. They're just trying to drum up a reason to keep the money."

"Yeah, but twenty million dollars *is* a lot of money."

Rusco had been surprised by Carlton's death, because in his experience, mean-as-a-snake, sons-of-bitches seemed to live forever. Carlton survived the strokes, but he became even more belligerent toward Anita and took to screaming garbled directives and profanities whenever she entered his room. This went on until he died.

As Carlton's chief legal counsel and go-to man, Rusco worked closely with him for over two decades and understood his depravities—flaws similar to his own—but in Anita's shoes, he'd have killed him a long time ago just to end the abuse. He couldn't see her doing that. However, not long ago a maid confided she was passing by Anita's bedroom and overheard her scream, "I just can't believe it...what a fucking bastard!" but never learned what Carlton did to provoke her.

Anita had a tough side, Rusco knew. After the child molestation episode with their friends' son, Carlton said she'd called him a "disgusting pervert" and refused to have sex with him. Things got so bad, a convenient accident for her was being considered when she retained the most aggressive attorney in Chicago and told Carlton he'd lose the shirt off his back, and his nuts along with it, if anything happened to her; documents containing everything she knew about him would be delivered to State and Federal attorneys and the *Chicago Tribune*. She added, "Then you can spend the rest of your life in the penitentiary with some HIV-infected stud's dick up your ass." *But kill him? I dunno... Yet, she's been pretty happy lately.*

Anita said, "Gene, you're right. The kids and I can use that insurance money, and I'd hate to have some nit-picking doctor screw things up on a technicality. Will you look into it? I know you helped Carlton out in the past when things got held up."

Rusco wondered how much Carlton had told her. Probably not much, since she wouldn't be asking for his assistance if she knew the full scope of the "help" he had given.

"I'll be happy to, but it may be a while before I get to it. We're swamped with work and all of my partners are backlogged."

"With me as the beneficiary of Carlton's will, and you as the Executor, I'm sure we can work out an arrangement that will allow you to get to it right away. Maybe ten percent of the insurance award?"

Rusco said, "I'll see what I can do," as he put on his best poker face and hid his emotions. He thought, *Here's this goddamn Hungarian gold digger, bargaining with me like hired help, and she doesn't have a clue about the millions Carlton and I stashed in the Panamanian bank accounts.* He almost bit through his tongue to keep from laughing—sixty-five million dollars unbeknownst to her or the U.S. government would be his after Brantel's investigation is completed.

He wanted to beat and rape her on the spot and fantasized that she'd probably enjoy it. One of Rusco's favorite sayings was, "Women are on this earth to serve as cock docks and have children," and although he wasn't bisexual or pedophilic like

Carlton, he was a sadist and enjoyed punching and strangling as foreplay, sometimes with tragic consequences. He accidentally killed a prostitute during his last trip to Thailand with Carlton; it didn't bother him, but the authorities went ballistic—the sex trade is the region's economic engine—and he was no longer welcome in the country.

The theft of funds from Solishe Capital Inc. had taken years and was rooted in Carlton's genius for achieving high returns on investments; his published results were on par with the nation's best venture capital firms. In fact, Carlton was better than that, particularly in the funds he personally managed, and he'd been able to skim off returns above the firm's averages without anyone's knowledge. The company's auditing firm, selected for greed, mediocrity, and dependence on SCI's annual fees, didn't raise any red flags, and investors were happy with their returns. Massive sums of money flowed into the firm from billionaires worldwide who wanted to benefit from Carlton's golden touch.

Shaving off tens of thousands of dollars here and there without detection required a deft touch, right up Carlton's alley, but routing the money through sham businesses and into the Panamanian account havens was difficult, and he needed help. So Carlton enticed his longtime attorney and friend, Gene Rusco, to assist him by offering a 50/50 split of the stolen money. It was an offer too good to be true for Rusco, and he jumped at the opportunity. A partnership was formed.

Money laundering was complicated and time-intensive, and it involved legal subtleties relished by crooked attorneys like Gene Rusco, especially when accounts were shared. The setup processes for the accounts required Rusco to be a cosignatory, a potential downside for Carlton's long-term health given Rusco's homicidal history. But Rusco was also in danger because Carlton loved money more than any friend's life. Understanding their mutual risks, they hired separate attorneys in Panama and agreed to lockout clauses for the accounts should either have an unexpected death. If death was caused by an accident, disease, or natural disaster, the other person would get all the money, but this would happen only after the decedent's lawyer in Panama City determined no shenanigans were involved.

On the morning when Anita found Carlton unresponsive in bed, she called Rusco as she followed the ambulance to the hospital, putting him in a dilemma: should he call to take possession of the accounts immediately or should he wait until Carlton's death was confirmed in the emergency department? He chose the latter to avoid any appearance of impropriety, a decision he'd regret.

Anita had given the night nurse, maid, and household staff the previous evening off, as she did sometimes, but her live-in male aide, Arthur, decided to stay at home. He heard her screams and ran to Carlton's room to see what was happening—as did the cook, the maid, and the daytime nurse, all of who had just arrived for work that morning. One look inside the room at the sallow, dusky body told Arthur all he needed to know. After calling 911 and trying to comfort Anita, he called the Panama City phone number Carlton had provided five years ago with a $20,000 promissory note for this purpose.

Carlton's Panamanian lawyer took the call and locked all the accounts within five minutes, easy to do in this digital age, ensuring Rusco couldn't access the money. The fact that a doctor had not confirmed Carlton's death wasn't a problem because legal disputes that might arise about it would take years to resolve, pleasurable years of large fees and bribes from the accounts for unscrupulous attorneys and judges to support their mistresses, prostitutes, opiate addictions, and other licentious behaviors. Carlton, expert in such proclivities, had known the timing of his demise would matter little in the Panamanian courts and focused his efforts on safeguarding the accounts until Rusco's innocence could be confirmed or repudiated.

The lawyer was familiar with Brantel Mutual and knew its miserly fastidiousness regarding policy benefits would save him endless hours of investigative work and difficult decisions: the company wouldn't pay a cent until it made sure Carlton's death was natural. He found himself in the enviable position of having little to do except collect exorbitant legal fees for fictitious work, continue his plush lifestyle, and let the findings of Brantel's investigation guide his decisions. However, a working lunch with Rusco's attorney was necessary because Rusco had called from the hospital as soon as Carlton was declared dead and flew into a shit-hemorrhage rage when told he couldn't access the accounts. He calmed down after being reminded the money would be transferred when it was determined he had nothing to do with Carlton's death but remained belligerent and insisted this should happen as quickly as possible.

Wary of Rusco's legal background and Brantel's reputation for thoroughness and efficiency, the attorneys decided to work together to protect their professional interests and prolong the judicial proceedings, at least until construction of their vacation homes in the mountains near Boquete could be completed. The more hours to bill, the better, and unlike Anita and Rusco, they'd get their money regardless of the cause of death.

The meeting at the Solishe estate ended before noon and they went their separate ways, Anita to visit her sisters and tend to household responsibilities—her usual activities—and Rusco to learn about the doctor from Southern University Medical Center. They had concluded he would be coming to the North Shore soon.

CHAPTER 11 – FIRST TRIP TO THE WINDY CITY

The direct flight from Raleigh to Chicago on Sunday morning was delayed for two hours. It gave Damen time to think about Carlton Solishe's death and the interviews he'd be conducting over the next five days. Brantel Mutual's investigators had learned a lot about the Solishes by accessing public and confidential computer databases, but certain information could only be obtained from human intelligence, face-to-face encounters that reveal facts, trends, and attitudes necessary for understanding motivations. In Medicine, this takes place during the physician-patient interview in a clinic or hospital, which Damen had done for years. This investigation would require him to step outside his comfort zone into unchartered territory and interview people in their homes, businesses, and elsewhere on the North Shore. It was the reason for this trip, and he had not slept well for the past three nights.

Chicago's O'Hare International Airport was one of the busiest airports in the world, an anthill of hurried passengers, airport workers, and honking vehicles whose fast pace creates the false illusion of chaos. In truth, it's well-oiled and efficient. Damen's black car pickup was smooth, and he arrived in his room shortly after noon where a heart-healthy lunch and the stack of files he'd requested awaited him.

He spent the rest of the day preparing for this week's appointments. He'd be talking with Anita's neighbor and walking mate, a tennis partner, co-volunteers at the Botanic Garden and Holocaust Museum, her two sisters, and the coroner who performed Carlton's autopsy. Anita was last. There would be two interviews each day, one in the morning and one in the afternoon.

Brantel had arranged the appointments. They contacted Anita and explained that Damen would need to talk with her and others for the investigation to progress. She was asked to talk with those she knew beforehand to encourage their participation. Anita agreed, figuring this would be evidence of her support for the investigation; plus, it might shorten the process and allow her to get the twenty million dollars sooner. Later, Brantel made follow-up calls to review why the interviews were needed, obtain consents, and schedule convenient times and dates for the meetings.

No one refused, so it was going to be a busy week for Damen, who would be conducting the interviews alone. He had a lot of questions for each person, most the same, some different, and decided on a familiar method to put his interviewees at ease and enable him to remember what he'd be told: medical interviewing 101.

From the first day they see patients, doctors learn a rote approach for introducing themselves and obtaining a medical history. It combines an introductory handshake with open-ended questions to determine why patients are seeing them. Damen's was: "Good morning Mr./Mrs. Jones, I'm Doctor Damen. What brings you to see me today?" Then, he asks routine medical questions in an easy-to-remember format.

Damen chose a similar approach for these interviews: "Good morning, Mr./Mrs. Jones, I'm Doctor Jack Damen and I appreciate your willingness to talk with me today." And after exchanging pleasantries, "As you know from the phone call by Brantel Mutual Insurance Company, Carlton Solishe had a large life insurance policy and the company has asked me to look into his death from a medical standpoint. That includes talking with family members, friends, and others, so thanks again for agreeing to meet with me... Please tell me how you've known the Solishes."

Mary Hollender, Anita's best friend, lived in a neighborhood behind the Solishe estate. Its multi-million-dollar homes were set among rolling hills, ponds, and landscaped gardens and were linked by groomed walking trails that stretched out to surrounding properties. Mary and Anita walked early every day sharing news and gossip before having coffee at one or the other's home.

Damen's interview with Mary was scheduled after one of these walks in the mid-morning, and he hoped she'd open up to him. *There's little she doesn't know about Anita and Carlton's relationship*, he thought, *so I'll try to stick with Mom's admonition, "It's easier to catch flies with honey than vinegar," and be gracious throughout the interview.* Mary, he would learn, planned to use the same technique for a different reason.

Arriving at the Hollender's home for his two-hour appointment, he was caught off-guard by Mary's cordial welcome. *This is weird*, he thought, *Anita may not get a lot of insurance money because of what I learn, and here's her best friend greeting me like a next-door neighbor*. It didn't take him long to figure out what was going on.

Mary had prepared some coffee, assorted biscotti,

and fresh biscuits with honey for his visit. They sat in her back sunroom, now emerging from the morning shade, and she extolled the virtues of living on the North Shore, their clean living, and eating organic foods. She talked endlessly about the health benefits of the honey they were eating—Damen admitted how tasty it was—until it became obvious she was stalling to avoid talking about the Solishes.

Damen was well versed in this tactic: many of his patients at Southern were skillful in evading discussions of sensitive personal matters. Anticipating a pre-arranged phone call that would draw Mary away from their meeting, he interrupted her.

"Mrs. Hollender, I hate to be rude, but could we talk about the Solishes? It's possible something could come up to shorten our meeting and I have a lot of questions for you."

Her face puckered like she bit on a lemon. "Sure, I'm sorry… I didn't mean to bore you."

Damen said, "It wasn't boring at all. Ordinarily, I'd like to hear more, but my time here at the North Shore is limited." He hesitated. "So, please tell me about Anita and Carlton Solishe."

"Okay, sure."

She began by describing her relationship with Anita and how much she values her friendship and that they walk almost every morning.

"We talk about all sorts of things, nothing too personal, you know, but about stuff that happens every day."

"What about Carlton?"

"We talked about him hardly at all," she lied. "I mean, we have since he passed away but not before. He got sick and that was a strain on Anita, but they seemed to have a good marriage otherwise."

Damen said, "What about after Carlton molested their friend's son?"

She frowned and sat back crossing her arms. "I didn't realize you'd know about that."

He shrank in his chair to appear less threatening. "Yes, in cases like this, insurance companies learn all sorts of things about their clients…and their families."

Mary said, "And their friends?"

He stared at her without a smile. "Sometimes."

The phone next to her seat rang. She said, "Excuse me," and put it to her ear.

"I'll have to do that later," she said to the caller and hung up. Her friendly demeanor was gone.

Her eyes narrowed, "OK, Dr. Damen, what is it you want to know?"

She revealed that Anita and Carlton's marriage was turbulent with frequent "highs" and "lows," even before the molestation, and that Anita was generally unhappy in it. Anita hadn't shared the specifics of arguments she had had with Carlton but often became emotional and teary-eyed when she talked about their relationship. Being the wife of a highly successful and immoral businessman who spent most of his time away from home, Mary empathized with her.

Damen had learned from Brantel's investigators that Chet Hollender, Mary's husband, kept a mistress in downtown Chicago not far from his office, convenient for midday trysts and semiweekly "business meetings" that required him to stay in the city overnight. Was Mary aware of this? Maybe so, maybe not, but it didn't matter. In their North Shore culture, this wouldn't be a marriage breaker as long as the arrangement was discrete and everyone's needs were being met: social status, attractive companionship, membership in exclusive clubs, glamorous homes, and plenty of money to spend on trips and other luxury items.

Infrequent sex and Chet's infidelity were small prices to pay for these rewards. Mary preferred sex with her longtime female housekeeper anyway, so she'd had a pleasing life over the past twenty years. Her suspicion that Damen knew this and other secrets fueled her newfound openness.

She continued, "After Carlton's strokes, Anita seemed to lighten up a bit."

Damen said, "Even with him being stuck in bed and requiring care twenty-four hours a day, seven days a week?"

"Well, it wasn't that bad for her—she had full-time nursing support so she didn't have to clean and change him or deal with his personal-care issues."

"I heard he was pretty demanding."

Mary said, "Yes, but she could limit her time with him whenever he got out of control. Even with his strokes, he understood if he was too miserable she wouldn't come to his room for a few days."

"Wasn't she worried he'd get mad and get a divorce or cut her out of his will?"

"No. She told me a neurologist doctor examined him and found he wasn't capable of making rational decisions or communicating thoughts. His last will was what counted and he had left everything to Anita and the kids."

Damen said, "Did Anita ever mention anything about her father?"

"Some."

"Anything about his suicide? You know, why he might have done it?"

Mary wondered why he was asking about that and what it had to do with Carlton's death... "Yes, but it was hard for her to talk about; she cried every time. All I remember is that she said he got swindled out of a lot of money, money he was planning to live on during the rest of his retirement. He went to the Chicago police and filed a complaint —that's how Anita learned afterwards what had happened—but nothing ever came of it. He was a proud man and never said anything to Anita or her sisters, and since his wife had died and wasn't there to console him, she figured he became overwhelmed about how he'd make ends meet and decided to end it all."

"Do you recall when Anita last talked to you about it?"

"Gosh, it's been a long time. Carlton had his strokes over five years ago and her dad died a couple of years before that, so it's been at least six years or so."

Damen glanced at his watch and said, "Thanks. I've got several other questions to ask you, so is it okay if we talk about some other things?"

Breathing deeply, she said, "Sure." This was different than what Mary had expected. Damen's questions were like those of a detective—nosey, like he was filling in the details of something he already knew. And he asked about a lot of things that weren't medical.

The interview went on until about noon, when Damen had to cut things off so he could make the short drive to the tennis club in time for lunch with Anita's tennis partner. He left with the information he had wanted from Mary, and as it would turn out, a lot more.

Thank goodness for responsible people, Damen thought, as the septuagenarian tending the entry gate of the North Shore Tennis Club directed him to the clubhouse dining room. Emily Collins, Anita Solishe's regular tennis partner, had communicated Damen's impending arrival and was waiting for him.

Emily was in her mid-fifties, trim, and tan despite the February weather. Light caramel and black-checked slacks and a tailored, black silk bomber jacket complemented her shoulder-length brown hair. She welcomed Damen with a firm handshake and direct gaze, making it clear she was accustomed to successful men and would not be intimidated.

After exchanging pleasantries and ordering his food, Damen got right to the point—he sensed Emily would appreciate it. From Brantel files, he knew her husband was the CEO of a large Chicago-based interstate trucking company and they had three sons in college. She didn't work outside the home and their daughter, a high school senior, lived with them.

Other than being a tennis fanatic, Damen thought she was as close to normal as any of Anita's friends and acquaintances. He was comfortable talking with her.

"I understand you and Anita have been doubles partners for the past eight years. Is that right?"

"Yes."

"Is she a good tennis player?"

Emily said, "She's really athletic and strong, and we won our age division city championship three years ago. I couldn't have found a better partner and we've grown pretty close."

"Did she talk much about her relationship with Carlton?"

"No, not really. We talked about a lot of things—kids, community goings-on, shopping, neighbors, that sort of thing, but not about Carlton. She never opened up with me about him other than when he got sick, although I told her a lot about my husband."

Damen said, "Could you ever tell when things at home might not have been going well for her?"

"It's interesting you ask that. She plays her best tennis when things at home seem to be going well and her worst tennis when they're not."

"How's her playing been over the past year or so?"

"Well, we haven't gotten into the City Finals since our championship, and the last six to eight months have been a struggle. She said everything was fine, but her game fell off quite a bit. I think the years of taking care of an invalid caught up with her and she just needed some time away. But then again, we're older and slower."

"Have you played since Carlton's death?"

Emily said, "No, not really. I called her and we've gotten together to volley a few times—I just wanted to take her mind off all the stresses and strains of his death—and I think it helped some. She seemed really grateful."

"I'm sure she was." Damen hesitated. "Do you know if she had another person in her life other than Carlton, either before or after his strokes?"

Emily looked hard at him. "I don't think so. She never mentioned anyone, and there are lots of opportunities here at the club. Men are attracted to curvy women in tennis skirts, especially her, and we've laughed at the lines used by the young and old guys who've tried to hit on us. No, Anita's a good girl and I think she's been loyal to Carlton despite his well-known transgressions."

Damen's eyes smiled at her unintended self-compliment. She blushed.

The Cobb salad and ice tea were excellent, and they continued talking for almost two hours before departing on good terms. He was sure Emily would be "volleying" with Anita over the telephone this evening to recount their lunch discussions.

Later that night after a much-needed nap and dinner, Damen typed his report and stared at the medical files stacked in the corner of his hotel room. Every morning he put them in the hotel safe to ensure confidentiality and compliance with insurance investigation regulations—they contained everything known, medical and otherwise, about the people he was interviewing. It was ironic that most of the information had been stolen.

For years the federal government had required clinicians and hospitals to use electronic health records, ostensibly to expedite billing and improve patient outcomes through shared access to medical data. This included collecting and storing personal health information in government and private databases through compulsory agreements between healthcare organizations and providers. When combined with all the non-medical personal information that had been collected for other purposes—banking, mortgage and credit card records, social media, phone and Internet communications—few aspects of a person's life remained secret. All Brantel had to do was contact unscrupulous sources with access to the desired databases, and the requested information would be provided within twenty-four hours; the sources enjoyed sizeable jumps in their discretionary incomes.

Damen read until after midnight. He didn't sleep well because of the ethics struggle he experienced from reviewing unlawful material in the files, but after some soul-searching and a hardy breakfast with two large coffees, he was ready for the next round of interviews.

CHAPTER 12 – VOLUNTEERS

*H*ow in the world, Damen wondered, *do sales representatives keep sane when they travel hour after hour to appointments that may, or may not, pay off for them?* Here he was, heading East on a four-lane highway in a rental car he didn't like, coffee cup in hand, morning sun in his eyes, bumper to bumper traffic, and the inactivity and boredom were killing him. *Hopefully, the interviews with Anita's co-volunteers will be worthwhile.*

The Chicago Botanic Garden covered 385 acres, had more members than any public garden in the U.S, and was an oasis of beauty and education for horticulturalists from around the globe. Anita had loved to grow plants and flowers since childhood, and because it was an easy fifteen-minute drive from her house, she began volunteering there shortly after moving to the North Shore.

Damen's appointment at the Garden was with Joanne Henderson, a volunteer co-worker who worked with Anita. The Brantel file on Henderson was thin: married to an accountant for thirty years, secretary for a local insurance company, and three unmarried adult children who lived in Texas, Colorado, and Oregon. She spent free time volunteering at the Garden and her church.

Joanne met Damen in the Visitors Center cafe, and they found a secluded table by the window overlooking an ice-glazed lily pond surrounded by green junipers and red winterberry. After his opening spiel, Joanne launched into a thirty-minute monologue about the history, merits, and beauty of the Garden, undeniable for sure, but not the purpose of the meeting. Damen interrupted as she gasped for air between sentences.

"I understand you and Anita volunteer here every two weeks or so."

"Oh, I'm sorry, I get excited and carried away by this place. Yes… Yes, we work together every one to two weeks."

Damen said, "Does she talk much about her home life? Or the relationship she had with her husband, Carlton?"

"No, not at all. I didn't even know his name until I read his obituary and went to the viewing."

Joanne leaped into a machinegun description of the viewing—people, flowers, pictures—and Damen had to redirect her back.

He said, "Is Anita a happy person, I mean, when you've worked together?"

"Sorry… Yeah, seems to be. Just like everyone else she has good and bad days, but overall she seems happy."

"No sadness after his death?"

That's a really stupid question, Joanne thought. "Yes, of course, but she seems to have recovered pretty well."

Damen continued for several minutes before deciding to take a different tact.

He said, "Does she have any favorite plant collections or areas here where she likes to spend her time?"

"Well, she loves and really knows about Rhododendrons. There's a unique and beautiful collection of hybrids here that grow well in our climate, and even some of the professors who teach here look her up to talk about them."

"Has this been a longtime interest of hers?"

Joanne said, "Ever since I've known her, but particularly over the past eight to nine years."

The conversation went on for another hour, but got bogged down, like a long walk in deepening mud. *Joanne seems kind and well-meaning*, Damen thought, *but she loves to hear herself talk...and her monotone is horrendous. Maybe I can get away from her by faking a seizure and falling through the window into the lily pond.*

Unable to take any more and realizing he would get no additional worthwhile information, he thanked her and excused himself so he could get to his "next appointment before lunch." After getting a double espresso, an ice-water face rinse, and a small lunch at the nearest Starbucks, Damen headed for the day's second interview and prayed for the strength to get through it without going nuts.

The Illinois Holocaust Museum and Education Center in Skokie, Illinois was dedicated to "preserving the legacy of the Holocaust" and was the result of efforts begun in the 1970s by Holocaust survivors following neo-Nazi activities in the area. Anita Solishe began volunteering at the Center, first in the library and gift shop, and now as a certified public tour leader in the museum. Since she was raised Catholic and there was no mention in her Brantel file of a conversion to Judaism, Damen was curious about why she chose to work there.

Deborah Hart, Volunteer Coordinator at the museum, met Damen in the Visitors Center and gave him a brief tour of the museum before they went in her office to talk. She was direct, loud, and animated—*Thank goodness*, thought Damen, *no need for a lily pond swim because of this one*.

Damen said, "So, Anita has been volunteering here for about twelve years and you've worked closely with her?"

"That's right, for the past eight years or so."

"One question I've got to ask is why you believe she spends so much time volunteering here. You're Jewish, is that right?"

"Yes."

"Our insurance company files indicate that Anita isn't Jewish and, pardon my frankness, I've wondered why she's interested enough in the Holocaust to spend a day here each week."

Deborah said, "It turns out we have many non-Jewish volunteers here, something that's confusing to people without a lot of knowledge about the Holocaust. Although six million Jews were targeted and killed because of their faith affiliation, millions of non-Jews were killed for a variety of other reasons. Anita loves her family and its heritage; she chokes up when talking about its persecution in Hungary during World War II. Her family immigrated to the

United States when she was a teenager, her parents and siblings, but not any grandparents or aunts and uncles. They were all dead, most after being rounded up and slaughtered by the Nazis. Some of her relatives may have been Jewish, but only a few, and she told me volunteering is her way to help prevent the cruelty seen in the Holocaust from ever happening again."

"Did she ever talk about her marriage or family?"

"Not much other than about her two kids. She is very proud of them, and we often exchange stories about our kids' accomplishments and awkward moments. You know, how parents do…"

Damen said, "What about her husband, Carlton Solishe?"

I wondered when he'd get to him, Deborah thought. "She never mentioned Carlton other than he was her husband and had some health issues. Nothing else, not a word about how they got along, and nothing regarding his death except acknowledging it happened when I offered my condolences. I live in a neighborhood a few blocks away from her and his name is taboo around there because of some pretty bad rumors. I felt uncomfortable saying anything more at the time, and she hasn't brought him up since then."

"What are the rumors that you heard?"

Deborah shifted in her chair. *He has to know about*

this, and I just don't like talking about heresay. "I'm sure you know all about it, but something to do with pedophilia and a friend's son. I heard the rumors and don't know anything more about it and really don't want to. If the rumors aren't true, there's nothing to discuss, and if they are, she's got a whole lot of problems that she'll bring up when she wants to."

"Although she shared very little about her situation at home, did you ever sense she was unhappy or frustrated with it?"

Deborah said, "Not really. She mentioned that Carlton was bedbound after some strokes and that he was sometimes difficult to manage, but that she had lots of help."

"And after his death?"

"No. In fact, it's horrible to say this, but she's seemed more relaxed since he's been gone. She's a beautiful woman with a great smile, and she gives excellent tours of the museum."

Damen said, "Did she ever mention her parents or siblings?"

"She didn't talk much about her mother except that they were really close. Her father committed suicide several years ago, a real tragedy, and it broke Anita's heart—I don't think she's gotten over it yet. She said he was a proud man and that, in her words, 'his soul was shattered' when he lost his retirement nest egg."

Deborah continued. "She talks about her sisters in Chicago that she sees every week or two, Julia and Rahel—I remember their beautiful names. After Carlton's death, and with her kids being away in school, I'm glad she has family nearby. Being alone after living with someone for years can be gut-wrenching."

From the information in Brantel's files about Deborah's bitter divorce five years ago, Damen knew she was speaking from personal experience.

The interview lasted another hour, and Deborah was full of information about the Holocaust and other related subjects. Walking to his car afterwards, he turned and looked back at the mausoleum-like gray building and thought of the pictures, artifacts, and memories it contained, horrid reminders of the immanent evil in humankind. He had to consciously shut out the demons as he thought of his own life and Beth—it was not a good sign. The investigation was beginning to weigh on him.

A walk in the nearby county park and a light dinner in a local Latin restaurant cleared his mind before he returned to the hotel to record today's events and prepare for tomorrow's interviews with Anita's sisters, Julia and Rahel. Later, after reviewing their files in light of what he learned today, he thought about how interesting it will be to visit and talk with them...interesting indeed...

CHAPTER 13 – THE SISTERS

Julia Niemec, Anita's youngest sister, lived in a Southwest Chicago neighborhood where small one- and two-story homes are separated by their driveways and maybe a narrow strip of scraggly grass. Her husband was an electrician and was away at work when Damen knocked on the front door.

A petite brunette in slacks and a crew neck sweater had let him in without shaking his hand or saying a word; she had high cheekbones and an unmistakable likeness to pictures of Anita Solishe. Wary and unsmiling, she made her feelings about Damen's visit clear.

"Doctor Damen, I wouldn't have agreed to talk with you unless Anita told me it would help the insurance company finish its investigation into Carlton's death and she could get the money from his policy sooner. You go ahead and ask your questions, I'll try to answer them, and then you can leave."

No phony airs here, Damen thought. He said, "I appreciate your honesty, and I'll make this as quick as possible." And he did, moving from question to question, issue to issue, without any covert attempts to gain her trust.

Julia sat with her arms crossed, back straight, and with a rigid face the entire time. She gave yes-no answers to Damen's questions until he pressed, then kept her explanations short. It was frustrating, but buoyed by years of interviewing resistant patients, he was able to get what he needed from her, and more.

While the answers to his questions were key, the living room where they sat was valuable as a window into Julia's life beyond the information provided in Brantel's files. The furniture and decorations—rugs, plants, knickknacks, and wall pictures—spoke volumes about her personality and preferences. Several pieces of Kalocsa, the colorful Hungarian embroidery, hung on the walls, and Damen commented on their beauty; Julia's curt response was, "Mother taught us how," and said nothing more, her attitude unchanged.

A cluster of family pictures were showcased on an embroidered doily that topped a corner desk. Damen recognized Julia's sisters, Rahel and Anita, and their parents, Istvan and Rebeka, from the files he'd reviewed; Carlton was in none of the pictures. Istvan's picture rested on a small, blue-white-blue striped rectangular embroidery with a partially-covered yellow Star of David in the center. He thought that was odd because the family were devout Catholics and made a mental note to look into it.

Damen thanked her as he left, but she didn't reply and closed the door with a loud thud and locked it. *Whew*, he thought, *that was painful*. He drove to a local playground where he could get out, take a stroll to stretch his legs, and try to make sense about what he'd learned.

Four themes had surfaced during the interview, repeated in Julia's answers like talking points: "Carlton was a mean, perverted man"; "He raped that eight-year-old boy and Anita had to send their children off to school"; "He was rich, but what a bastard—nobody liked him"; and "Anita is a sweet person and didn't deserve this." Based on the information in Brantel's files, this was nothing new, but Damen was surprised by Julia's conspicuous reiterations and deep-seated hatred of Carlton. *It's one thing to dislike someone because of what they've done to you or someone you love*, he thought. *It's another thing to harbor a primeval hatred, an intense loathing that permeates one's being, like I saw in Julia as her eyes narrowed, her voice deepened, and her face became distorted whenever she talked about Carlton.* It was something Damen easily recognized—

he had felt it in San Francisco when Beth was assaulted.

Ground fog is forming in the investigation, he pondered. *Maybe I can clear it up when I talk with Rahel this afternoon...*

Rahel Kozma lived in a condominium building that backed up to the Chicago "L" train system Orange Line, about a mile from her sister Julia, and agreed to talk with Damen while she was off work for a dentist appointment. Damen waited in the foyer of the three-story, 1970s red-brick complex and occupied himself by speculating about the other names on the intercom panel until she buzzed his entrance into the elevator.

Unit 303 was on the third floor, and Rahel welcomed him with a guarded smile and handshake. Like Julia, she was a brunette and resembled pictures of Anita, but her features were more rounded and less severe. The aroma of freshly brewed coffee indicated she was not planning to rush through their discussions.

The suite had two bedrooms, two bathes, and was consistent, Damen felt, with Rahel's job as office manager in a local insurance agency. It was neat and clean, with some expensive furniture from an earlier time before her ex-husband, a purchasing agent for a construction company, began buying favors from the city's night workers and left telltale green stains on his undershorts. She couldn't forgive him, and their subsequent divorce netted her enough money to purchase the place.

The living room where they sat smelled of flowers, coffee, and cinnamon, and both had relaxed by the time Damen got to his key questions.

He heard again, as he did from Julia, that Carlton was a perverted child rapist, a wealthy and hated son-of-a-bitch, and that Anita was a wonderful person who deserved better. However there was more, and it came out after Damen shook his head and said, "I can't understand why they stayed together."

Rahel said, "Carlton didn't want a divorce because Anita told him he'd be broke by the time she got done with him. And he knew she had information that would send him to prison."

So, Anita knows about some of Carlton's dealings, he thought. "What kind of information?"

"Stuff about his business. I'm not sure exactly what, but Anita told me the FBI and Federal Courts would get everything she knew if anything ever happened to her."

Damen interrupted, "What'd she mean, 'if anything ever happened to her'?"

"She didn't say, but Carlton was such a shit that she wouldn't put anything past him."

"And she kept living with him?"

Rahel said, "Doctor, as you know, people stay in unhappy marriages for many reasons: money, prestige, personal needs of other types." She stared at Damen with a look that Damen recognized from previous encounters with women who found themselves alone and desiring companionship.

Damen felt vulnerable—Rahel was attractive and smelled all woman—and quickly steered the conversation back to Solishe's business dealings.

He said, "Did she tell you anything more about the 'information that would send him to prison'?"

"No, except that the guy who always hung around Carlton, Rusco's his name, would also be in big trouble."

"How did Anita hold up after Carlton's strokes?"

Rahel said, "She did OK at first, after learning there would be no financial issues. A new person was hired to run Solishe Capital for the short-term, Carlton had humongous disability insurance, and eventually the business was sold for a lot of money. It kept them in their home with all the medical support help while he was alive, and she got the rest of it after he died.

"The problem was that Carlton became a bigger pain in the ass after his stroke than he was before. He couldn't understand what was being said to him and wasn't able to talk, so all he did was scream and wave his left arm whenever he wanted something. You can tell mean screams from just wanting screams, and eventually all his screams seemed to be mean, no matter what Anita did for him."

Damen said, "Was she glad when he died?"

"I don't know if I'd say that, but her life became quieter, that's for sure!"

"What did you feel about Carlton?"

Rahel blurted, "I hated him—he killed our father." She flushed, let out a long breath, and rolled her eyes. "Wow…I'm sorry… Dad hung himself, no doubt about it, but my hate won't go away and my mind keeps saying that Carlton put the rope around Dad's neck. But thinking that is crazy… I mean, Anita found out from the police after Dad died that he had met some guys at a bar in his neighborhood, and they convinced him they were financial big-shots who could turn what little retirement money he had into a fortune. So he gave them his money and they disappeared. Afterwards, there he was, alone with barely enough money to live on and without Mom to talk with—she died from breast cancer a few years before that

—he was too damn proud to let any of us know what had happened to him." She teared up and started to silently cry.

Damen felt like an intruder into her personal moment and looked away. His eyes found the family photographs on a nearby bookshelf. As at Julia's, they had been placed on an embroidered doily; a blue-white-blue rectangular embroidery with a yellow Star of David at its center was beneath Istvan's picture. Damen realized how important ancestral heritage was in this family, and Istvan appeared to hold a special place in it. He wondered if this was how most patriarchs were viewed in Hungarian culture—

Rahel sniffled loudly and continued talking about Carlton. "He was such an arrogant ass and always thought he was better than us. The first few years after Anita married him, we'd get together as a family and Carlton would look down his nose at us. You'd think that with him and Dad being the only guys, he'd talk about 'man things' with Dad. But no, he treated him like a peasant, and sometimes like he wasn't even there."

Damen said, "Did you and Anita ever discuss this?"

"No, I just couldn't bring it up with her. I mean, how do you say to your sister, 'Your husband is a fucking asshole and is treating Dad like shit.'?"

"Do you believe she thought Carlton was being disrespectful or mean to him?"

"No. When times got rough for Dad, Carlton gave Anita extra money so he could stay in his place, visit our brothers, things like that. She thought he was really nice to him."

They talked for another hour, and although Damen was learning new information, he sensed Rahel was holding something back. But, he thought, it had been a long day and maybe he was tired. It didn't help that he was having difficulty concentrating: Rahel was a flirt and he was physically attracted to her, something she instinctively knew. A soft, longer-than-needed handshake when he left sent Damen the clear message that she would welcome a meeting with him unrelated to Carlton Solishe's death.

Damen drove back to the hotel and had an early dinner. Afterwards, he typed up his daily report and reviewed several of the files again. The ground fog in the investigation had not been cleared by Rahel's interview; it was thicker, and he called room service for a large pot of strong coffee. It was time to reconsider his assumptions.

He'd brought Jasper along on the trip for just this situation and filled him to his hairline. Three hours later, his mind was dancing with new possibilities about Carlton's death as he crawled into bed and thought about tomorrow's interviews with the coroner and Anita Solishe.

CHAPTER 14 – THE CORONER

Lake County, Illinois, uses a coroner's office to perform autopsies and assist in the investigation of deaths. Unlike medical examiners, coroners are elected to their positions and don't have to be physicians or have knowledge about criminal investigations. It was unusual that Lake County's current coroner was a physician and pathologist with training in forensic pathology. With a staff of seven deputy coroners, the office had earned the respect of local and state law enforcement officials for the detail and quality of their autopsy findings. The chief coroner conducted Carlton Solishe's autopsy.

Dr. Daniel Lange was a thoughtful man who did his homework after Brantel Mutual Insurance called for an appointment with the person who performed Carlton Solishe's autopsy—him. Brantel explained this was in reference to a large life insurance policy and that Dr. Jonathan Damen would like to discuss the autopsy findings. Lange Googled "Damen, MD" and learned he was a tenured, full professor at Southern University Medical Center.

The academic rank of professor is reserved for those who've published numerous scientific articles, received research grants, and achieved national recognition for their academic accomplishments. Damen seemed young for the rank, but Lange found he had authored over 120 peer-reviewed manuscripts and received seven National Institutes of Health (NIH) research grants for breakthrough work in autoimmune and malignant thyroid disease. He also found a magazine article about Damen: "The Doctors' Doctor at Southern." Putting it all together, Lange realized this appointment would test the limits of his medical expertise.

Damen too had done his homework and learned a lot about Daniel Lange from the Brantel file he read last night: where he grew up, his educational history, including medical school and residency, his fifteen years as faculty at the University of Chicago, and the alcohol and cocaine-fueled behaviors that decimated his family life and academic career. After intense counseling and drug rehabilitation, Lange had resurrected his personal life and remarried, redirected his career into forensic pathology, and eventually was elected to his current position in Lake County. It paid well, had regular hours, and was free from the teaching and publishing pressures present in first-tier medical schools and research institutions.

The similarities between them—smart physicians, abuse of alcohol, personal demons, and shattered relationships—were on Damen's mind as he arrived at the Coroner's Office shortly before his 9 a.m. appointment.

Anticipating a long meeting with a learned academic, Lange had cleared his morning calendar. He did not envision the rugged, black-haired man who walked in and introduced himself, a person who might intimidate others but not him. Like former military combatants, alcoholics, and others who've walked comparable, painful paths in their lives, there was immediate recognition and an unspoken familiarity that allowed them to move through the usual social courtesies without delay and into the autopsy findings.

Damen said, "I read your autopsy report and it was very detailed and complete."

"Thank you."

"Are your reports usually this extensive."

"No, just the ones where I can't determine a cause of death…and those where there may have been a reason for third-party harm."

Although he knew the answer already, Damen

said, "Which was it for this one?"

Lange answered bluntly, "Both. A lot of nosy people live in Lake County and unsavory information—confidential—about its movers and shakers spreads like wildfire whenever it's leaked. As I'm *sure* you've already discovered from your investigation, Carlton Solishe had a reputation as a ruthless businessman and a pedophile. When I couldn't determine a cause of death, I went over everything again to make sure he wasn't murdered."

Damen was amazed how many people knew of Solishe's sexual proclivities given the private nature of the legal proceedings that forced his perversions outside the U.S.

"And you didn't find any evidence of that?"

"None. I found the expected findings in his brain from strokes, and evidence of vascular disease throughout his body due to hypertension and high cholesterol levels, but nothing else of significance."

Damen said, "I read that the toxicology report didn't indicate any unusual drugs or medications. How extensive was the testing?"

"It was a basic screening panel, along with levels of his medications, diltiazem and lorazepam, and both were fine."

"Were the levels from his blood or eyes?"

Lange said, "Everywhere."

"Do you still have vitreous samples from his eyes?"

"Yes, we usually freeze and save two samples of vitreous for a year after death."

"OK...," Damen continued. "The only thing in your report I couldn't figure out were the skin findings in *External Examination*. You mentioned the skin on his back was mottled in places, and you even took biopsies of the mottled areas and adjacent normal skin."

Lange said, "Yeah. I still don't know what the discolorations were from. I haven't seen it before, a circular mottling on his back toward the sides, not in the center of his back. It looked like something you'd see from egg-crate foam mattress covers that are used for bedbound patients, but not quite. He had a few early skin ulcers from just laying in bed all the time, but these areas were different. The biopsies just showed small, localized infiltrates of white blood cells consistent with mild inflammation. I took pictures of the mottling—Would you like to take a look at them?"

"I sure would. Your pathology slides are digitalized, right?"

"Of course. I e-mailed the slides to pathologists I

know at the University of Chicago to see if they could come up with something, but they had nothing to add."

Lange and Damen talked for another two hours about the autopsy findings and the stresses of teaching and doing research at large medical centers. After reviewing the pictures of Solishe's back and recalling he'd seen something similar several years ago in a patient at Southern who had received medication through transdermal skin patches, Damen bid goodbye to his new friend with the understanding he could have access to a tube of the eye vitreous and digital copies of the skin biopsies.

Damen had lunch at the Latin restaurant where he ate dinner following his interview with Deborah Hart. Anticipating he would need a mid-day break to relax and consider what he learned from Lange, he'd packed Jasper in the car this morning and was glad he did. The lunch crowd was different than the evening clientele and Damen loved it.

Tieless in his shirtsleeves, making a mess eating chips with chipotle guacamole, and draining the face mug twice while he thought, Damen melded with the hodgepodge of patrons whose knit caps, beards, semi-washed jeans, and customized beverage containers broadcast, "I am different." It was perfect for thinking outside the box before his interview with Anita Solishe. *A short drive to her home,* he mused, *and maybe some more pieces for the puzzle.*

CHAPTER 15
– INSIDE THE SOLISHE ESTATE

It was a cloudless afternoon, sunny and cold, and a film of shiny water was all that remained on busy highways after the weekend snowstorm. Damen turned at the wrought iron "S" and drove up the plowed private road to the small guardhouse and gate that prevented unwanted visitors further access into the property. He felt like an intruder entering Anita Solishe's world, and he hoped the interview with her would go well

A mud-spattered Vespa scooter leaned against the side of the building. The man who met him, an unmistakable brawler, seemed out of place in this genteel neighborhood, and Damen wondered if this was an omen for the rest of the day.

"Hello, I'm Dr. Jonathon Damen and I have a one thirty appointment to speak with Mrs. Solishe."

"Yes, *Doctor*, Mrs. Solishe is expecting you."

It wasn't the tone of his voice that bothered Damen but his eyes. He recognized those eyes—he'd seen plenty of that kind in Columbia—dangerous eyes of a person who would do whatever it took to remove unwanted obstacles. They were the eyes of a killer.

Damen spoke as the gate was raised. "Thank you Mr. …"

"Kelly, Jimmy Kelly. Mr. Kelly to you."

Damen was not afraid of any man, but he'd need to keep an eye on this one. Jimmy Kelly was in his fifties, six feet tall, and 220 pounds, with a big neck, an angled nose from fighting, and large mitt-like hands. A lifelong friend of Gene Rusco, Carlton's attorney, he'd guarded the Solishe estate for the past fifteen years and was waiting to meet the doctor who Rusco said, "Is trying to screw Mrs. Solishe out of a lot of insurance money." Kelly's allegiance was to Rusco, who got him this job, but Anita Solishe had always treated him with kindness and respect, and he took pride from intimidating undesirable callers.

So that's how it's going to be, Damen thought, and he grinned. "Thank you, Mr. Kelly."

As Damen drove up the drive, Kelly thought how much he'd like to smash the smart-ass doctor's smiling face.

The drive twisted through the woods before opening into the circular parking area in front of the mansion. *This is what real money gets you*, Damen thought as he walked up the broad circular steps to the columned porch where Anita Solishe's personal aide of twenty years, Arthur, met him.

"Dr. Damen, welcome. Mrs. Solishe is expecting you." He motioned toward the open front door.

"Thank you."

They walked across the foyer's polished marble floor, past its elegant curved staircase, and into an adjacent parlor. Several small logs burned in the fireplace and warmed the seating area that was perpendicular to it. Anita Solishe and a tall man with graying hair stood up from their chairs.

Damen was struck with how attractive Anita was. The family resemblance with Julia and Rahel was strong, but Anita had a lighter complexion, smoother skin, and was dressed to accentuate her thinner figure. She exuded sexuality unusual for a woman her age, and Damen felt an attraction similar to what he experienced with Rahel. He suspected she had talked with her sisters after their interviews and wanted to be alluring for hers. She was.

She shook his hand. "Dr. Damen, I'm Anita Solishe, and this is our family attorney Gene Rusco."

The Brantel files on Gene Rusco were thick and described a ruthless and smart attorney, who, over many years, managed to keep Carlton Solishe out of prison. He'd had personal scrapes with the law, including unproven links to the murders of three of Carlton's business competitors, but he was never brought to trial for anything. However, the files couldn't convey the aura of danger behind Rusco's veneer of civility. He looked like a monitor lizard in a Brooks Brothers suit, and as they shook hands, Damen imagined a forked tongue flicking out of his narrow smile.

The three sat down, Damen on a small leather couch opposite their chairs. He moved two Kalocsa motif throw pillows to make room and said with admiration, "The embroidery on these is beautiful."

"Thank you," Anita said pridefully. Without wasting any time, she continued, "Dr. Damen, Brantel Mutual has informed us that you've been hired to look into Carlton's death. I don't understand why! He had a heart attack and two large strokes, and died after five miserable years stuck in bed being totally dependent on others for care. He's finally at peace and we're trying to move on with our lives, but now there's a delay in settling the insurance policy he paid a pretty penny for."

Rusco handed her a tissue and she dabbed at her eyes.

She said, "I'm sorry, but this has been hard on all of us." She hesitated. "I'd like to get things wrapped up as soon as possible...I hope you understand... Now, what can I do for you?"

Damen said, " I know this is a difficult time for you. I'm here because it's standard procedure for life insurance companies to have independent medical investigations of deaths associated with large policies. Mr. Solishe's was one of the biggest written by Brantel Mutual. All I need today is to ask you some questions about Mr. Solishe's condition after his strokes, and particularly, the days and evening leading up to the day he died. First, I'd like to talk about the morning you discovered he had passed away. I've read the Brantel files but need to confirm what's in them and to clarify a few facts."

"OK," Anita said, "but it was horrible, and it's still horrible whenever I think about it." She frowned and clenched her hands in her lap.

"I understand, and I'll make this as brief as possible," Damen said with compassion. After hesitating, he continued, "The files indicate you found him unresponsive when you checked on him that morning. Is that correct?"

"Yes. I would usually come in to see him first thing in the morning after the nurses had cleaned him up and given his tube feeding—he felt better when he had something in his stomach. The nurses weren't there that morning because I gave them the previous night off. I did that sometimes so they could have a break.

"I came in to do the cleaning and hang the bag with his tube feeds, but he looked pale and didn't open his eyes when I called his name. His face felt ice cold, so I shook him hard. He wouldn't wake up…I knew he was gone, but I called 911 anyway. They took him to the emergency room where he was pronounced dead, and the Medical Examiner's office was called to do an autopsy."

Damen said, "Did he get his diltiazem and lorazepam the day before?"

"Yes, the nurses gave him the diltiazem in the morning and I gave him the lorazepam that evening."

"Did he have any other prescription or over-the-counter medications that day?"

Anita said, "When he seemed to be in pain, moaning or making noises for no reason, we'd give him some Tylenol, but none that day or night."

"Any other medicinal or nutritional products?"

"No."

Was there a subtle change in her demeanor when she said this? Damen's sixth sense, honed by thousands of patient interviews, was on edge. But perhaps it was nothing.

"Had he vomited?"

"No."

Damen said, "Did anything else appear unusual that morning? For example, were the sheets or blankets messed up or his bed clothes?"

"No, he was just laying there, like I mentioned."

"What about the day and night before. Was he acting well? No signs of him getting another urine infection or his bed sores getting worse and infected?"

Anita said, "No, he seemed his usual self. He was awake most the day, and he let the nurses know when he wanted something by making noises and moving his left arm and leg, like always."

I wonder what he's after, Anita thought, as Damen continued his questioning over the next hour. She felt he was good-looking in a rough sort of way and wouldn't have guessed he was a doctor. But he talked like one, made her relax, and asked the harder questions in a nice way.

Rusco also wondered what Damen was after. *This guy's different for a doctor,* he thought, *and there's toughness behind his manners and disarming voice.* His questions seemed harmless, and he could have gotten most of the answers by reading the reports compiled after Carlton's death—So what was the purpose of this interview? Probably he was just jumping through the necessary administrative hoops to get a handsome paycheck. On the other hand, maybe he was looking for something else, but if so, he wasn't pushing.

Anita answered most of his queries without hesitating, helped by occasional input from Gene Rusco. Hoping to get a sense of her truthfulness and to assess her relationship with Rusco, Damen had decided to ask "softball" questions at this meeting. By the end of the interview, he felt both goals had been met. Tougher discussions would come later.

The afternoon light was fading when Damen drove down the long driveway; he found the guardhouse empty. There was no scooter in sight, the gate blocked the drive, and the building's door was locked. Because of trees and the thick underbrush, Damen couldn't drive around the gate, so he was going to have to crawl through the window to reach the switch to raise it.

Before he left, Jimmy Kelly had cracked open the window and smeared some mud and deer scat on the windowsill to piss off Damen when he crawled in. Damon didn't see or smell it until he was halfway through the window, and it *did* piss him off —he was sure Rusco and the household staff had keys to the guardhouse and the muck was a present just for him.

Once inside, he hit the button to raise the gate but not before photographing the last four months of the visitors log. He also put a wet, used plastic cup from the trashcan into a Ziploc evidence bag.

Damen got back to his hotel, washed off his coat and pants, and not being a procrastinator, called the head of Brantel's Solishe investigation team, Sean Murphy. He'd learned an immense amount from the interviews over the past four days and most of it made sense and fit into recognizable patterns of events and relationships, but some of it did not, and he wondered if the files Brantel had provided for him to read could have been incomplete. Murphy picked up the phone on the second ring and, after exchanging pleasantries, Damen shared what was bothering him. "Sean, there are dynamics and issues related to the Solishe family that I don't understand. For example, Anita's sisters, Julia and Rahel, detest Carlton Solishe a lot more than I'd expect from what I've read about him. Is it possible there's information regarding him that's not in the files you've given me, you know, additional details that could help me in my part of the investigation?"

This guy's really sharp, Murphy thought, *and he's being tactful about asking if we've kept anything from him.* After a moment of silence, he said, "Dr. Damen, a couple of weeks ago we sent investigators to Thailand to learn more about Carlton's activities over there, and they were able to purchase a photocopy of the personal diary he had taken with him on several of his visits; the location of the original is unknown. It cost us a lot of money, but it has material in it that may address some of your concerns. We haven't sent it to you because its content is so sensitive from a legal perspective that our boss, Mr. Castelman, ordered us to keep it under wraps unless you had questions pertaining to what's in it. I'll arrange for a copy of the diary to be hand-delivered to your home in North Carolina after you return. It's for your eyes only and will need to be kept in a secure location."

"Thanks, Sean, I appreciate it." *I knew there had to be more information,* Damen reflected, *but hadn't realized I'd have to pry it out of them. Maybe the diary is so unique, though, that it had to be this way.* "And there's something else." He described the blue-white-blue embroidered rectangle with the yellow Star of David in its center that he saw beneath Istvan's picture at Julia's and Rahel's. "Your files indicated they're devout Catholics, yet both had their father's picture on a Jewish insignia. I'm going to draw a picture of it and email it to you tonight. How about asking your team to research it and try to figure out what it might be?"

"Will do. Anything else?"

"Yes, a couple of other items. I'll be sending a plastic cup to you for DNA identification, plus there are a few additional things I need the team to look into." Damen gave him the necessary information. "I'll let you know if I think of anything else. Thanks again," he said and hung up.

Damen spent the rest of the evening writing notes for his report. Tomorrow, he'd catch an early plane to Carolina in time for afternoon rounds with his team at Southern. *It will be nice to get home*, he thought, *and away from this complicated mess.*

CHAPTER 16 – THIRTY YEARS AGO

It had been before daybreak when the two young toughs left Youngstown, Ohio, heading to the noon football game in Buffalo. As soldiers in the notorious Ohio Mob, they rarely got the weekends off, so when their capo said he wouldn't need them until Monday, they decided to drive three hours and see the Buffalo Bills play the New York Jets. The capo didn't like "his boys" leaving Ohio, so they didn't mention to anyone where they were going.

After parking and buying general admission tickets, they found two vacant box seats near the field and enjoyed drinking beer after beer while watching a typical Bills-Jets game, a nail-biter, won this time by the Bills with an overtime field goal. The Bills fans, almost everyone in attendance, went wild—screaming, dancing, hugging—and in the moment, the two men realized they were missing something: women and sex. The stadium was located outside the city center so there weren't any street walkers available, but that wasn't a problem because they were able to find what they wanted at the nearby hospital.

Adina Garrone's breath rose like smoke in the cold, wet Buffalo night as she walked to the parking lot. It had been a long shift on the pediatric cancer ward, one that tested her limits as Head Nurse and as a human being. But it was over now, thank goodness, and she was headed home to begin preparations for her daughter's birthday tomorrow. The whole family would be coming over for the celebration and there was lots of cleaning and cooking to be done.

She got to her car and fumbled in her purse for the keys. As she found them—it had taken extra time because her hands were so cold—there was a noise behind her. She started to turn, but the fierce blow on the side of her head robbed her consciousness. Unaware of being thrown into the back of the small cargo van and having her white nursing pants torn off, she was mounted and penetrated by the ringleader of the two rapists who wasted little time before rolling off, breathless from his assault. The second thug, thickset and strong and stoked by alcoholism and voyeurism of the first, was more brutal. His animal-like thrusts were violent, accompanied by deep pleasure groans and alcohol breath, and he released deep inside her. She awoke feeling the pain and terror of the moment and screamed. His sledgehammer fist broke her nose and he strangled her.

"It's a shame. She was a good lay," he said to his predecessor, now smoking in the driver's seat of the van, "…nice tits and a tight twat." He pushed her partially nude, lifeless body to the side and pulled up his pants.

The narrow-faced smoker said, "Yeah. And now, you dumbass, we have to get rid of her."

"And where we gonna do that? Let's just leave the bitch"

"No way. Remember, we ain't here, right? Anyways, I've got the perfect place and they won't find her until we're home."

They cackled like the teenagers they were a decade ago and drove off, convinced of their invincibility.

The driver had been to Buffalo before and remembered a deserted road and creek where they could throw the body. It was raining hard so there wouldn't be any telltale tire tracks or footprints. No traffic, one minute to get the body out of the van and over the bridge railing, an uneventful drive back to Youngstown that night, and a perfect crime had been committed. Or so it seemed.

They didn't say a word to anyone about where they'd been or what they'd done, and it was fortunate for them that they didn't. Within two days, police in Buffalo and the Mob throughout New York State had been mobilized to find who killed Rochester Mafia boss Antonio Cirazzi's daughter. The efforts were fruitless, however, and her murder became a well-known cold case because of Cirazzi's notoriety, the generous reward he had offered for information leading to her killers, and tabloid-page speculation about what might happen to the rapists if they were ever identified.

Learning their victim's name and fearing a horrific revenge if discovered, the perps extricated themselves from the Youngstown Mob two years later during one of its internecine battles. Over the ensuing decades, they remained in close contact and never far apart—their survival depended upon it. The secret could never get out.

CHAPTER 17 – A TEAM IN THE PITS— AND REVELATIONS

The week Damen was in Chicago had been rough on Team 2, and they were tired. The winter weather and an influenza outbreak in the Southeastern U.S. resulted in the highest numbers of admissions to Southern Medical Center in the last ten years. Dr. Charles "Chuck" Asherton had covered for Damen, but he wasn't as hands-on and the team had found they couldn't rely on him for backup during the busiest times. The residents were working long hours, it had been cloudy and rainy the entire time, and patients were dying despite excellent care. An overall bleak week.

Damen met his senior resident, Dr. Joon Kim, in the 5 North conference room. "Joon, it's good to be back," and they shook hands. "Chuck just debriefed me and it looks like the team has had a lot of sick people, real train wrecks."

"Yeah, it's been a hell of a week. All the outlying hospitals are unloading their flu complications as soon as they turn sour—pneumonias, heart attacks and heart failures, strokes—and I can't blame them. I mean, they don't have the ability and staffing to take care of these folks so they have to send them somewhere, and we're 'it.'"

"Any avoidable disasters?" asked Damen.

"No, the team's working well. Julie's done a good job supervising when I can't do it, and Mark and Michelle are solid, especially Michelle who works hard and is smarter than heck. Nyquim and Holly are among the best fourth-year students I've seen. We've had a few medication fuck-ups, but they were discovered early so no harm was done."

"Great."

Kim hesitated. "We missed you… Dr. Asherton is good, but he has a lot of research and administrative responsibilities, and he doesn't dive in when the shit hits the fan. I remember the last time we worked together and you did some admissions to take pressure off the team. It helped a lot. We could have really used you here this week."

"How are you doing?"

"Tired, but I've been there before so it's not too bad."

Damen said, "You sure? As you know, I feel our team's mental health is essential for good patient care."

"Yep, I'm fine for now."

"How about the others?"

Kim said, "Not so good, especially Mark. He's been away from his wife and son a lot this month and misses them. He says he's so tired when he gets home all he wants to do is go to sleep. And several of the patients who've died were his; he's bummed out about that, even though his patient care has been excellent."

"What about Julie and Michelle?"

"I didn't tell you about this before, but Julie has been dating a PhD physics student on main campus for a few months and really has the hots for him. She hasn't seen him much since our team started because the service has been so busy, and when she does, she's exhausted. She's been supervising well, and her patient care has been good, but she's starting to get abrasive to patients and everyone else. I've talked with her about it."

"Good."

"On the other hand, Michelle's been in her element. The busier she is and the sicker her patients, the more she loves it. No kidding, as the country folks around here say, she's as 'happy as a pig in manure.' And she's major-league smart. Once she gets a year or two of clinical experience under her belt, I think she'll be one of the best residents ever at Southern."

"Even better than you?"

Joon smiled. "Maybe."

Damen said, "Med students doing OK?" He figured they were since they didn't have to stay in the hospital beyond six p.m. each day. Also, their patient care is closely supervised and they wouldn't feel responsible for any bad outcomes.

"Yep, fine."

After talking a few more minutes, Damen and Kim met the other Team 2 residents and medical students for brief afternoon "rocket rounds," where lingering patient problems and issues that come up during the day are addressed. They were happy to have him back, but their tired eyes and long faces broadcast the collective depression that's often seen in medical teams after caring for large numbers of extremely ill patients. In before sunrise, home after sunset, work through the day dealing with sick and dying patients and their families; then evening paperwork, phone calls, and emails so the next day is clear for more of the same. It was a perfect recipe for burnout. Each team member had one day off per week to go to the bank or grocery store, sleep, clean up, and lay eyes on loved ones. It was doctor boot camp, the traditional rite of passage from medical school to providing comprehensive patient care.

Damen sat down with the team following rounds and addressed them. He said, "I'm sorry I've been gone this week. Joon and Dr. Asherton told me you've had lots of sick patients, and that you've done a great job caring for them. They also told me everyone's getting exhausted. I know you have more gas in your tanks, but I think it will be beneficial to have a break to get human again, to spend time with friends and family, or just to be alone for a day without any responsibilities. We have an all-consuming life here in the hospital, and people who haven't done this can't understand the stresses it places on us and those whom we love.

"Joon will work with each of you to pick a day off this week in additional to your usual day off. I'll cover your team responsibilities on those days. My only requirement is that you truly take the day off. I know how anal all of you are and that your first temptation that day will be to check in to see how your patients are doing. Forget it. This is a guilt-free day off for you to enjoy. God knows, you've earned it!

"Joon, I'll need names and days off at teaching rounds tomorrow morning." Damen stood up and left the room.

Kim and the rest of the team looked at one another and were quiet. They'd never heard of an attending at Southern doing this before; it was always "work until you drop and personal life be damned."

Michelle was the first to speak up. "Joon, are we such a sorry group that he feels we need a break?"

"No, not at all. When I worked with him last year, he helped the team at the end of the first month on service but more subtly. He would do one to two workups each day for whomever was doing admissions because of the depression funk that hits all teams about a month into the rotation. Damen told me it's hard to give patients good care when we're not taking care of ourselves or our loved ones."

Joon looked at the team. Mark Mestule's and Julie McKenzie's eyes were welling up, and the rest of the team stared ahead in silence. It was time for a break, any type of break. He said, "We'll figure out our days off during work rounds in the morning."

The next three weeks were a blur of sick patients and long days in the hospital, but Damen's elbow-to-elbow relief work paid off: Mestule seemed happy, McKenzie wasn't cranky or horny, and laughter and teasing returned to the team meetings. Damen got home late most nights, tanked up on joe from Jasper's head, and reviewed information he'd requested from Brantel's investigators plus whatever other new discoveries they'd made, related to it or not.

It's like living through a paper avalanche, Damen mused, as new files were delivered to him almost daily that contained facts and intelligence squeezed through cracks in the confidentiality laws for private, government, and industrial databases. *To access some of these materials, people had to have been bribed and businesses and private homes burglarized. How else could they have gotten this stuff?* Nothing about Carlton Solishe seemed to have been off limits—bank accounts, medical records, credit card histories, international travel records and transactions, overseas accounts, photocopies of files from a private investigator he had used.

The crown jewel among the new information was a copy of Carlton's diary. Sean Murphy, the head of Brantel's Solishe investigation team, had kept his promise and the diary copy with related information was delivered by courier to Damen's home three days after being requested. Its contents revealed that Carlton had been an extreme narcissist with a perverted infatuation about the immoral and evil deeds he had committed: he wrote them all down for future turn-ons. After an orgy in Thailand, or after shafting someone in a business transaction, he'd record the details in his diary. Whenever he wanted to get sexually aroused, he'd read a choice morsel or two.

The hookers he frequented in Thailand had noticed his strange foreplay—reading the small book with the hand-drawn title *Cervantes* while snorting cocaine—and thought there might be something useful in it. One night, after Carlton had passed out following sex, coke, and other drugs, they opened it and discovered it was his putrid diary, not a Kama Sutra-like masterpiece. Their pimps photographed its contents, read every sordid detail, and planned to extort him during his next visit to Thailand; unfortunately for them, he had the strokes before he could return. The pimps eventually lucked out, though, when Brantel's investigators went to Thailand asking about Carlton. The prostitutes he used mentioned the diary, and notwithstanding it had been more than five years since he'd been there, the pimps had saved the photocopy of the diary. Brantel paid thirty grand for it and got an autobiographical account of Carlton's peccancies, turd by turd, including most of the illegal, immoral, and unethical things he'd ever done. The location of the original remained a mystery.

The files delivered to Damen day by day weren't limited to matters pertaining to Carlton—the investigators had looked wherever Damen asked, and that included a comprehensive re-dive into the lives of Anita and her family, friends, and acquaintances; everything they had collected about them, private tidbits from every nook and cranny of their lives during the year before Carlton died, were made available for his review. Murphy's team had even unearthed a possible explanation for the blue-white-blue embroidered rectangle with the Star of David in its center that Damen had noticed beneath the pictures of Julia's and Rahel's father, Istvan, at their homes. They found it resembled an insignia of the Jewish Brigade, a military unit of the British Army during World War II composed largely of Jewish soldiers that had participated in the Italian Campaign in 1945; the unit had also aided Holocaust survivors during the later stages of the war and shortly afterward. For a brief time following the German surrender, some members of the Brigade were reported to have conducted revenge killings of Nazis who had committed atrocities against Jews.

Of the information Damen had requested, only the DNA studies on Jimmy Kelly's guardhouse cup remained outstanding. Sean Murphy called and said they'd forward the results to him as soon as their team received them from the outside lab performing the tests.

The late night and early-morning hours spent

reading the materials that had been sent to him —new information that complemented the files he'd digested at the beginning of the investigation —enabled Damen to visualize a complicated mosaic, a picture in his mind of Carlton Solishe's life and final months, weeks, and days...and of the people around him. It was all coming together and seemed to be pointing to one hard-to-imagine set of scenarios. He needed to think it through and, if it held up, decide what on earth he was going to do about it.

A complicating factor was that the long, arduous hours working and teaching in the hospital and studying the files into the wee hours of each morning had been exhausting, and sleep deprivation was never good for Damen. Without fail, it fostered introspection and soul-searching, looking backward into his life and brooding about every bad thing he'd done in the Army and since then, misdeeds that seemed worse whenever he was tired. *It was a mistake to participate in this investigation,* he had told himself last week, *but I'm okay*. After reading more of the files and losing additional sleep, he wasn't so sure; he let the team know *he* needed some time off and went home early one afternoon just to sleep and relax on his front porch. Muffy, his neighbor Mrs. Greumach's dog, was busy chasing cars as usual—he liked the scruffy mutt because its large, protruding eyes reminded him of his patients with hyperthyroidism— and provided an island of normalcy in the whirlpool of the current situation as he wondered, like he had many times before, how long this would go on before a car permanently won the competition. *That's me in this investigation*, he reflected wearily, *running hard to stay ahead of the cars in my conscience*...and he dosed off for four hours.

When he awoke, he called Emmi—they had made it a point to touch base at least twice a week whenever he was away from the river—and the sound of her voice invigorated him. *I love this woman*, he smiled as they talked, *and she's always been supportive, no matter what. It will be great to see her again after this investigation wraps up.* From her tender words and tone of voice, Damen knew she was looking forward to being together with him again too.

The hours of rest and talking with Emmi cleared his mind, and afterwards, as he re-examined the facts and his conclusions in the case, he realized confirmation bias, the interpretation of information and data in ways that support one's personal beliefs or values, might have distorted his reasoning and latest determinations. Although he'd been aware of Carlton's evil ways, Damen's ingrained hatred of "bad people," controlled through years of psychotherapy, had resurfaced amid his sleep-starved revelations from the diary. He worried he had come to despise the man and that this could have affected his judgements about what happened to him...and why. He needed more corroboratory information, so he called Michael Lange, the Lake County coroner, and asked him to send a vial of the eye vitreous from Carlton's autopsy; Lange shipped it immediately. Its analysis validated Damen's suspicions and provided the final piece in the puzzle.

Professor Emeritus of English Edgar McCutcheon was schmoozing with customers at the Bard Owl, his four-star restaurant, when he broke away to greet Damen and Team 2 as the maître d' escorted them to the private dining room. He'd grown fond of Jack and Beth when they dined there each month, but he rarely saw Jack after the divorce despite attempts to lure him back with promises of free Oban single-malt whiskey. So he was ecstatic when he learned Jack had reserved the Windsor Room for a dinner party of seven. *Ah*, he thought, *Jack is getting the divorce behind him after all these years.* He would have been disappointed to learn Damen was there because of a lost bet.

The trip to the Bard Owl originated during outdoor grilling on the first warm weekend of the Carolina spring. Southerners love to grill anything —steaks, chicken, corn, you name it—and Damen invited each medical team he'd been working with to his home at least once to discuss interesting cases over grilled concoctions and drinks. Resident physicians, medical students, and fellows looked forward to the food and intellectual stimulation from Damen's medical puzzles and, for non-teetotalers, the added stress-reducing effects of judicious wine and whiskey.

Having recovered from the previous grueling month, members of Team 2 were enjoying themselves like well-fed puppies when Damen began talking about the case of a fifty-eight-year-old male who died unexpectedly five years after having a heart attack and two debilitating strokes. "Why did the man die?" was the question to the group. As Damen revealed information that pointed to the cause of death, he expected the team to deduce the answer. But they did not, and weren't even close.

This was unsettling because whenever Damen discussed medical problems with his young doctors and they failed to reach agreement, it raised the possibility *his* conclusions weren't correct. However, he was sure of himself this time and, because they were so off base, he felt the team would never get it right. In a moment of Oban-induced arrogance, he bet no one could figure out the cause of death. And if someone did, he'd treat all to dinner at the Bard Owl. Ideas, with supporting logic, were to be written and submitted to him within one week.

It was not a good wager for Damen.

Six theories: five wrong and one right. *This dinner is damn expensive*, Damen thought, *but worth every penny*. Recalling her mischievous smile when she turned in the report, Damen chuckled as Michelle Lewis, red-faced but grinning ear to ear, explained its conclusions to her inebriated and howling team colleagues.

It was time to return to Chicago.

CHAPTER 18 – REALIZATION & DANGER

The weeks following her and Rusco's meeting with Damen at the Solishe estate had been eye-opening for Anita as she became aware of the scope of Brantel Mutual's investigation into Carlton's death. Based on what her sisters, friends, and co-volunteers told her about Damen's meetings with them, she had expected Brantel to quickly wrap up loose ends and pay out the policy. Instead, its investigators conducted additional person-to-person interviews and online research—invasive and wide-ranging probes into private matters—which Anita discovered by chance.

It began at the local pharmacy where her sister Rahel picked up prescription refills. She looked forward to picking up her refills because of George, the senior pharmacist. He was in his late fifties, married, and had four grown children and passels of grandchildren. He also had appreciative eyes that caress-searched Rahel every time she went in, so she dressed provocatively and enjoyed his near-drooling attention to her. It would never lead anywhere, but she still liked the thrill of being able to turn a man's head with her looks. On this day, she was sporting the red lipstick, tight jeans, low bodice, high-heel tart look, and George began to blush and sweat after one glance.

He panted, " Hi, Rahel. How's today treating you?"

"George, it's good seeing you. I'm just picking up my monthly prescriptions. You're looking fit and well, so life must be good."

"No complaints. I'll get your prescriptions ready, but come over here for a second." He gestured toward the end of the counter.

"Something happened the other day and I thought you should know about it. Some guy from an insurance company that's investigating Carlton Solishe's death came in and asked me about your prescriptions. I'm not sure how, but he knew what medications you're taking. I told him right off that our medical information is confidential and none of his business, but he was persistent and left only after I threatened to call the cops."

Rahel said, "What'd he look like?"

From the description, it was not Jack Damen.

Thanking George until he turned red, she left after giving him a sinful smile, a close view of her gaping cleavage, and a hips waggle he'd dream about for weeks. She called Anita when she reached her car.

After hearing Rahel's story, Anita wondered what the heck was going on. She had asked everyone to cooperate with Damen, to answer his questions, and now someone was nosing into her family's private business. Since it hadn't been Damen who visited the pharmacy, it must have been someone else who worked for Brantel. Or maybe not. She needed to find out who was behind this and what else they were looking into; and she needed to warn people in case it was a blackmailer or some other scam.

She sat down to think. After a cup of tea and a few quiet moments, she had an idea, and unbelievably, it was thanks to Carlton. *He was such an egotist and smartass*, she thought, recalling the discovery of his diary eighteen months ago. It held his daily thoughts and deeds—twisted chronicles of a perverted and evil life—recorded like a philosophical antithesis to the Book of Sirach.

He'd glued on a fake, hand-inscribed cover titled *Cervantes* and put it among the books on his office bookshelves figuring it would never be discovered. Anita had been cleaning out the office and stacking books for a local library fundraiser when the diary fell open, revealing Carlton's handwriting. Its despicable contents were imprinted on her brain, but there also was the name of a private investigator that might be useful now. She called and made an appointment to talk with him.

Three days later, Andrew Dillon watched Anita enter his office. She was wearing high heels and a tailored light blue dress. He shook her hand. "Good morning, Mrs. Solishe. It's nice meeting you. Please have a seat." He motioned to the chairs surrounding a small table, and they sat down.

"What brings you to see me today?"

"Well, Mr. Dillon," Anita said, "after my husband, Carlton, died, I found the name of your business in his records and it stuck in my mind. I've got a problem now that needs investigating, and I don't know who else to turn to."

Dillon said, "Do you know the nature of the cases I worked on for Mr. Solishe?"

"No," Anita lied. "Just that he paid for your services several times over the past few years."

That's good, Dillon thought, *because one of the cases involved her father*. He never learned what Carlton did with the information he unearthed, however, so he didn't have any ethical qualms about hearing Anita's issue. Besides, she was good-looking and rich.

Anita told her story, beginning with Carlton's death and ending with Rahel's visit to the pharmacy. "I want to learn who's behind the pharmacy visit, and if it's Brantel, where else they're sticking their noses."

Dillon was having a lull in business and accepted the case. Two weeks later, he handed her a comprehensive report and a bill for $20,000. Bribes had consumed $5,000; the rest was for him. The Brantel investigative team didn't learn about the report until much later; they were impressed with his techniques and findings and planned to outsource future Chicago-area work to him.

Anita read every detail in the report and began to understand the multi-headed scope of the investigation. Damen was one component, an important one, but faceless others from Brantel were dissecting every aspect of her life and those of her family and friends. She shared the situation and her concerns with Gene Rusco over lunch.

She told him about Rahel's experience and that she'd hired Andrew Dillon to look into Brantel's activities.

Shit, Rusco thought, *how'd she know about Dillon?* Then he relaxed, knowing Dillon was tight-lipped and wouldn't discuss any previous dealings with Carlton. If he had, Anita wouldn't be talking with him today.

"Gene, it turns out they're investigating my sisters and all my friends. I think they're trying to find any way they can to screw me out of the money. They called this morning, but that's the first time they've contacted me since Dr. Damen's visit. With all they're looking into, I should have heard from them before now."

As she shared Rahel's story and other details of what Dillon discovered, Rusco realized Damen's initial interviews with everyone had preceded the recent uptick and re-direction of Brantel's investigative activities. *That fucker!* he cursed to himself. *If I don't get the millions of dollars due me in Panama, I'm going to kill that son-of-a-bitch. Screw it, I'm going to kill him anyway and dump his dead, medical superstar ass in the landfill. After he disappears, let's see how the investigation goes.*

"Oh, and Gene, Damen is coming here next Friday to meet with me."

Rusco thought, *Perfect...*

CHAPTER 19 – GOING FORWARD AND REACHING BACK

It had been a brutal winter and Chicago was defrosting after a final snowstorm, with mounds of gray sludge, muddy puddles, and residue from ice salt everywhere. Damen hated the thought of going there, if only for a long weekend—eight hundred miles south in the City of Medicine, azaleas were in bloom and the dusky morning fragrances of spring welcomed each day—but the trip to talk with Anita Solishe couldn't be postponed. He knew how Carlton died and needed to have an in-depth discussion with her about what he'd found and how it could affect the $20 million-dollar insurance policy payout. He'd be on his way at the end of the week, but first he needed to take care of a messy, last minute detail.

The results of the DNA analysis from the Solishe estate guardhouse cup that he'd sent to Sean Murphy at Brantel arrived yesterday and he had to make a decision: be a good citizen or step into darkness again. Ghosts from the past haunted him as he thought about it overnight, but for him there was no choice. After all, debts are debts.

He dialed the Rochester number he hoped never to use again.

"Yeah," the elderly female answered with a thick accent.

"Hello, I'm Dr. Jack Damen and I need to talk with Mr. Cirazzi."

"He can't come to the phone right now."

"Would you please tell him Dr. Jack Damen, who he knows from Rochester and San Francisco, would like to talk with him. Please ask him to call back at this number."

"I'll give him the message."

"Thanks."

As before, Damen's phone rang about five minutes later. "Jack, it's good hearing your voice. I didn't think I'd ever get another call from you. How's Beth doing these days? I hope Pineview Gardens is working well for her."

Knowing their conversation was being monitored and stored somewhere in a government supercomputer, Damen was measured with his words. He told him about Beth's mental ups and downs and the wisps of progress she was making; however, it was doubtful she'd ever leave there. And without giving specifics, he thanked Cirazzi again for his financial help at the Gardens and for everything he did for them in San Francisco.

Cirazzi said, "Jack, life's about relationships. You went the extra mile for Donny in Rochester and saved his life. I can never repay you for that." After other pleasantries, he paused. "You haven't mentioned why you called today."

"Mr. Cirazzi, I need to talk with you in private and was calling to find out how that might be arranged."

"Face to face? I'm slowing down and don't travel much anymore. Is this something you can share with Donny? He's taken over the family businesses in Chicago."

"Sure. It turns out I'm flying there at the end of the week."

"Perfect. You'll hear from us. Be safe, Jack." Cirazzi hung up.

Surprised at the quick ending to their conversation, Damen assumed he'd phone back sometime in the next couple of days.

Three days later, Thursday night, Damen checked in at the North Shore Hotel where he had stayed previously—he had not heard from the elder Cirazzi since they talked. The box he sent from Durham awaited him, along with a message from Donny that he'd join him for breakfast at 7 a.m.

Damen hadn't had time during the call to mention where he would be staying in Chicago. Tomorrow was getting interesting.

CHAPTER 20 – CHOICES

It was before sunrise on the North Shore when Damon met Dominic Cirazzi in the hotel restaurant. It was a meeting to partially repay a debt, obligations—past and present—related to Beth that he couldn't escape, thoughts of which reminded him almost daily about his dark side. Combined with the latest discoveries from Carlton Solishe's diary and other sources, Damen knew this was the beginning of a long and difficult day that would be capped by wrangling discussions with Anita about Carlton's death, and there would be danger. He was prepared.

The waitress guided him to the secluded table where "Donny" awaited. A tall, handsome man with black, gray-speckled hair welcomed him with a firm handshake. "Dr. Damen, it's been a long time."

"Mr. Cirazzi, it sure has. Please call me Jack."

"And me, Donny."

Donny was wearing a black blazer with a gray sport shirt open at the neck, the tracheotomy scar from the Rochester ICU in full view. This was done for recognition, but it wasn't necessary because of Damen's near-photographic memory. Other than some additional weight and normal aging, Donny hadn't changed much over the years.

Two muscular men were having breakfast at another table just out of earshot. They didn't look like police.

Damen said, "I appreciate you taking the time to meet with me. I thought I'd have to fly to Rochester to talk with your dad in person, but he told me he was slowing down and that you're now in Chicago; it turns out I'm working on an insurance case here. He helped me and my wife a lot during a bad time in San Francisco and with nursing home expenses since then, and although I can never repay him, I think he'll have a great deal of interest in what I'm about to tell you."

Donny said, "My dad told me all about San Francisco as well as your experiences in the Rangers. And, what's happened since San Francisco. You're a unique doctor…"

They ordered, and Damen discussed the generalities of the insurance case without betraying confidential information about the Solishes, their friends, or families. He handed Donny a large manila envelope. Their food arrived as Donny opened it and began reading. He stopped eating halfway through his eggs and sausage and looked up at Damen.

"Why are you giving this to me instead of the police?"

"Your dad feels I saved your life at Rochester General, but even so, he went above and beyond to help my wife and me in California. I know what it's like to lose a loved one to sexual predators, and I feel I owe this to your dad."

Donny said, "My father's never gotten over Adi's death… He says the hope of catching her killer is what keeps him alive. We put a hundred thousand dollars aside twenty-five years ago as a reward and it's accrued to about five hundred thousand. It'll be yours if this is true."

They spent a few minutes talking and finishing their breakfasts, then went their separate ways. Each was anxious to get moving. Damen figured the Cirazzis would act quickly, so he drove immediately to the Solishe estate; Donny called his father in Rochester and ordered his troops into action.

Lead pipes are great, thought Jimmy Kelly, as he awaited Damen's arrival. The snow had melted, the sun was breaking through the morning clouds, and he whistled an uneven tune in anticipation of this morning's pleasures. Rusco had called him two days ago and told him Damen was causing trouble—"The fucker is trying to gyp us out of a lot of money"—and that he needed him "to disappear" when he came to visit Mrs. Solishe that Friday. Kelly had never questioned Rusco's orders no matter what the task, so he found an old plumbing pipe to smash the smart-ass doctor's skull and brought it with him to the Solishe guardhouse. He figured it would be easy because doctors were wimps from keeping their noses in books their whole lives. All he had to do was trick him into getting out of his car.

Damen pulled off the main road and drove toward the guardhouse and gate just beyond the clearing.

"Good morning, Mr. Kelly. I have an appointment with Mrs. Solishe this morning."

"Good morning, Doc." Pointing toward the front of the car, he said, "Did you know your right front tire is almost flat? You won't make it to the house unless it's filled up."

Spotting the pipe against the guardhouse, Damen opened the car door and jumped out, surprising Kelly with his quickness. Swiveling to grab the pipe, Kelly turned back toward Damen and found a Kimber .45 centered on his heart. He froze. "Shit…"

Damen snarled, "Put it down, Cutozzo."

Shocked by the use of his given name, Jimmy Kelly dropped the pipe. "Wh... What did you say?"

"You heard me, Cutozzo. Don Cirazzi knows you raped and killed his daughter thirty years ago, and he's coming for you. You better start running..."

Pale and overcome with terror, Jimmy sprinted for his Vespa scooter and raced down the driveway away from the estate. He didn't get a thousand yards before a black car sideswiped him and two men threw him in the trunk hog-tied and sped off; his worst nightmare was beginning.

Damen holstered the Kimber cocked and locked. His internal alarms about danger had been on target and he felt he knew who was behind it—Rusco. He reached through the guardhouse window, hit the button to raise the gate, and drove to the house thinking about breakfast and Jimmy's probable fate. *Maybe I should have called the cops instead... but what's done is done*, and another questionable decision found its way into his mental regrets file.

He rang the front bell, and Arthur opened the door a few minutes later.

"Oh, Dr. Damen, I'm so sorry. Jimmy didn't call from the guardhouse, and Mr. Rusco said you might be a few minutes late."

I'll bet he did, Damen thought. *Disposing of a corpse takes time, and it would be evening before anyone raised concerns about me missing the appointment.*

Arthur directed him across the marbled foyer, past the staircase, and into the parlor where he'd met with Anita and Rusco during his first trip. The room was immaculate, wood burned in the fireplace as before, and Damen wondered what, if anything, ever changed in Anita's daily life.

Voices and footsteps approached. Anita had wanted to talk with Rusco before her meeting with Damen, and they just finished having coffee when Arthur notified them of Damen's arrival. Rusco hid his surprise from Anita, who was unaware of his deadly scheme, and they walked to the parlor together.

Damen shook Anita's hand. "Mrs. Solishe, thank you for meeting with me again." He turned toward Rusco's narrow face and angry eyes, and shook his hand. He lied, "Gene, it's nice seeing you again"- Rusco's freezing handshake and strained smile had revealed the source of Jimmy's plans.

Leaving Anita and Damen to their private meeting, Rusco excused himself and called Jimmy's phone. It rang and rang and transferred to voice mail. He tried again—same thing—and then drove down to the guardhouse. The gate was open, and Jimmy and his scooter were nowhere to be seen. *Some-*

thing is wrong, Rusco thought, *very wrong*.

After Rusco left, Anita sat down and faced Damen across a small coffee table where Arthur had left water, tea, and ginger cookies.

"So, Dr. Damen, how's your investigation going and what can I do for you?"

Damen said, "Mrs. Solishe, I've pretty much completed my investigation and I'd like to share some of my findings with you. The evidence indicates your husband did *not* die of natural causes."

Anita gasped. "What are you saying? That someone killed him?"

"It appears that way."

"Well… Well, how could that be? I was the only one in the house with him that evening except for my aide, Arthur, and he's been with us for years. Wait a minute," she laughed, "Are you saying that I killed him? Oh, I get it: you and the insurance company want to scare me out of getting the twenty million dollars!"

Anita was smiling, but her hands were clenched with barely suppressed rage. For a moment, Damen thought she was going to attack him. However, she took a few deep breaths and regained her composure.

"Carlton paid a lot of money for his life insurance policy, and I've cooperated with your investigation despite its endless delays. Now you show up and imply that I killed him. Frankly, Dr. Damen, that's a bunch of crap! I was married to him for eighteen years before he died, and although he was an unusual man, I loved him—we raised two children and had some good times. But go ahead, tell me what you've found...then I'll call my lawyer and you can go to the police with your fantasy." She rose and plucked a pen and small pad from the bookcase as if to write notes and primly sat down.

Damen continued, "Mrs. Solishe, you stuck with Mr. Solishe through a lot: verbal abuse, insults, the rape of your friends' son, perhaps molestation of your children, and the prostitution and pedophilia in Thailand—"

"How do you know about that?" Anita interrupted.

"It was discovered during our investigation. You had good reasons to divorce him, but you didn't, and you cared for him after his strokes. I figure it was when you found and read his diary, and the details of how he manipulated your father into hanging himself, that you decided to kill him."

Her eyes widened and her mouth slackened, just for a second. She said, "What diary? My father?"

"The small book, *Cervantes*, that Mr. Solishe carried with him everywhere—Thailand, for example—

and in which he recorded the perverted and cruel things he did. It described how he hired Andrew Dillon to investigate your father's finances, then conmen to steal his retirement savings. To top it off, Mr. Solishe detailed how he reveled in Istvan's subsequent depression and suicide, the emotional pain you suffered, and how he was able to manipulate your grief for his own sexual gratification… The rotten bastard finally got to you, didn't he?"

Anita's face paled, then reddened. "You're out of your mind."

"I don't think so. Your family's the most important thing in life for you, and while you couldn't prove he molested your children, you read his account of how he took pleasure in destroying your dad to hurt you. So, you and your sisters decided to kill him."

Anita's stare hardened.

Damen began to go over what else he and the Brantel investigators had discovered—secrets in Carlton's diary and constellations of information about Anita, her sisters, friends, and acquaintances—that supported his conclusions. Anita vehemently denied his accusations and repeatedly threatened to expel him from the house, but did not, and she listened until he finished. The meeting lasted almost ninety minutes, and their faces were hard to read when they emerged from the parlor.

As he headed for the front door, Damen thought, *She repudiated everything I said, despite the strength of the evidence, so what she'll do next is anyone's guess.* However, he had given her a good option at the end of their conversation, a win-win for both of them: how she could stay out of prison, preserve her family's reputation, and relinquish her claim to Carlton's insurance policy and walk away with even more money. The determining factor would be whether she believed what he had told her. He said, "I'll plan on coming by next Saturday morning at nine a.m. to see what you've decided."

Anita watched him leave, her face emotionless. She returned to the room alone and closed the door. Leaning against it, she contemplated their meeting and after a few minutes started making phone calls.

As Damen walked out onto the porch toward his car, he found Rusco waiting for him.

"Hi, Gene."

Rusco said, "Dr. Damen, did you happen to see Mr. Kelly when you drove in this morning?"

"Yeah. We talked briefly and then I drove up here."

"So, he was there at the guardhouse?"

Damen said, "Sure. Why?"

"Well, I can't find him now and that's not usual."

"Wish I could help you."

Rusco watched as Damen strolled to his car and detected a telltale bulge in his blazer behind the right hip. *The bastard's carrying a gun*, he thought, *and has to know something about Jimmy's disappearance.* He walked inside and called the groundskeeper to search the woods around the guardhouse.

CHAPTER 21 – HOLDING ON

They were waiting for him in the hospital classroom: Joon Kim, Julie McKenzie, the first-year residents Mark Mestule and Michelle Lewis, and the medical students Nyquim Berry and Holly Jones. Winter had faded into spring since dinner at the Bard Owl, fewer patients were in the hospital, and the team was well rested. That is, everyone except Damen, who slipped through the door, mumbled greetings, and plopped into a chair.

The early morning coffee and Cream Delight doughnuts, courtesy of Kim, softened the bright lights and frequent interruptions by nurses about the team's patients. Licking sugar flakes off her fingers, McKenzie proclaimed, "Nothing's better than doughnuts and joe after you've been up early and working hard for a few hours." As if in agreement, Damen swigged down a cup of coffee, ate a large chocolate glaze in three bites, and was eying another.

Mestule quipped, "Dr. Damen, they didn't feed you much in Chicago, eh?"

"No," he chuckled, "just hotel and restaurant food, the stuff that plugs your coronary arteries and shortens your life."

Berry said, "Sounds good to me, though!"

They all laughed and were glad Damen was back. However, his face had changed over the weekend: it seemed grayer and he looked exhausted—the toll of his side project was showing. Noticing this, Kim took the lead for rounds.

After a few lighthearted comments, he summarized what had happened with their patients during the weekend, then asked the other team members to review each patient in detail. It was a welcome relief for Damen who had been typing a preliminary report for Brantel nonstop after arriving from Chicago late Friday; he'd averaged less than three hours sleep per night since then.

The team went to see patients on 5 North and met again in the late afternoon to tie up loose ends. Damen, who had managed a quick cat nap in the hospital doctors lounge during lunchtime, sat down with Kim afterwards to discuss patient problems and the team.

"Joon, congratulations! It's a lot different than when we first rounded in January."

Kim said, "It sure is…they know the patients well and have excellent care plans for them."

Damen added, "And the team seems well rested and happy."

"Yeah, Julie's doing great. She and the physics PhD student seem to be working out. The others are good too: Mark and his wife have reached a truce about his time away, Michelle is dating an older insurance salesman, if you can believe it, and Nyquim and Holly aced their exams and got into their first-choice residencies for next year—they'll be here at Southern in Internal Medicine.

"That's great! What about you? Have you made a decision?"

Kim smiled. "Yes, I've decided to follow the example of the famous Dr. Damen and go into endocrinology. So you can expect a request for a recommendation."

Damen said, "It'd be my pleasure. Great news! Just let me know how else I can help."

"Thanks." Kim looked uncertain but then asked. "How are you doing?"

Damen hesitated. The Chicago investigation had been agonizing because of its connections to Columbia, San Francisco, and his divorce from Beth. Every night since Friday, he'd fallen asleep thinking about his past and questions that arose from his recent decision regarding Jimmy Kelly. *What kind of man do my choices make me? What is it inside me that makes ending a life so easy? My life is devoted to healing the sick and being a positive member of society, so why do I constantly find myself on the dark side of the coin?*

These weren't new questions. He had paid his psychiatrist at Southern a fortune to identify the personality aberrations that fed his dark choices and had spent countless hours on behavior-modification techniques to contain them and let his soul move on, but the internal demons were gnawing away the bars of their cage again. He prayed every day that he could hang on for a few more weeks without sliding backwards into the fog he experienced after Beth's brutal ordeal in California.

"Thanks for asking, Joon. It's obvious, isn't it? This case in Chicago has really taken a toll on me, but it's about to wrap up and I'm going to be one happy camper after it's put to bed."

Damen paused. "Are you asking because I'm not doing my job for the team? I need to know."

"No, things seem OK… We can tell you're bothered by something, but your teaching's been great, as usual."

Damen said, "Be sure to let me know if things seem to slide."

"I will."

"Thanks."

They shook hands and went their separate ways.

Damen walked to his office, happy to be back at Southern. Warm weather had returned, there were a manageable number of patients, and the team was doing well. But his thoughts kept going back to the North Shore of Illinois and Anita Solishe. He was anxious to learn what she had decided.

CHAPTER 22 – ANITA'S DECISION

It was Friday night at the North Shore Hotel, and until one hour ago, Damen had been looking forward to a restful sleep before his meeting with Anita in the morning. Brantel's investigators had informed him that she verified the financial windfall she'd receive from the option he proposed at their meeting last week, so he anticipated she would waive her claim to Carlton's policy and accept the deal. However, Gene Rusco might have screwed things up. *Life's dramas are fueled by relationships and changing circumstances*, he thought, *and the envelope I just received could spell trouble.*

The front desk manager had recognized Damen when he checked in—the pleasant, unassuming doctor from North Carolina who left a heavy book-size package in the hotel safe at the end of his stay last week; unbeknownst to the manager, it contained Damen's Kimber .45. He retrieved the package and handed it to Damen, along with a large manila envelope designated for him that a private courier had dropped off an hour ago. It was closed with tape and addressed to Gene Rusco, with "Confidential" stamped on the front and back. *This has to be from Donny Cirazzi*, Damen thought, *but how does he know Rusco? And, is Rusco expecting the envelope? Anita also? ...Crap!*

Sleep ended up being a three-hour wrestling match with unanswered questions and painful memories. Damen finally gave up. Exhausted, he took a cold shower, got dressed, polished off three cups of room service coffee with eggs, bacon, and toast, and drove to the Solishe estate.

The new guard, a recent retiree from the Highland Park Police Department, was expecting him and opened the gate. He motioned toward the house, returned Damen's nod, and noticed his frown and icy blue eyes—*the doctor's having a bad day*, he thought—but missed that Damen was driving with his left hand and the right hand wasn't visible. The right hand was holding the Kimber; after his encounter with Jimmy Kelly last week, he had come prepared for anything.

The winding drive was beautiful this morning, speckled with purple, orange, pink, and white among the hardwoods and pines, and a cloudless blue sky above. Damen soaked it all in and tried to relax so he could put on his smiley face. He drove into the circular courtyard at the front of the house, got out, and rang the bell.

Gene Rusco opened the door. He was leaning forward with narrow eyes and a set jaw, and said in a sarcastic tone, "Dr. Damen, so good to see you."

It had been a rough week for Rusco, and he blamed Damen for it.

Since Carlton's death, Anita had been lonely and called Rusco almost daily for advice regarding legal matters and to talk about random issues. The calls stopped after Damen's visit last week, and he didn't know why until they met on Thursday, two days ago: she'd learned about the secret accounts in Panama and how to access them from Damen. She told Rusco half the money was hers.

He laughed and said, "What do you mean, 'secret accounts' in Panama?"

Anita said, "Gene, cut the bullshit." She rattled off the account numbers, the amounts in each, and the names of the banks.

Rusco's jaw almost hit the floor. *I can't believe this*, he thought, *What else does she know?*

She continued. "You and Carlton had it all figured out: both of you live and you split the money whenever you like. If one of you dies from natural causes, the other gets the whole amount. But you didn't do your homework, and neither did those Panama City attorney hacks you hired. It turns out that buried in Panamanian law is a statute that relatives have beneficiary rights to these accounts. Most attorneys are unaware of the statute because the accounts are set up by crooks whose next of kin never know the money's been stashed away. When I learned what the two of you had pulled off, I filed for Carlton's shares and now they're mine."

Rusco snapped, "You're crazy as hell and don't know what you're talking about—"

From living with Carlton, Anita knew how to deal with bullies and cut him off. "You still have your shares, and if we work together, no one will be the wiser. It would be unfortunate for both of us," she said with a cold stare, "if the Illinois Attorney General becomes aware of our accounts and how they were funded. And, Gene, that will occur if anything happens to me or my relatives. I know how the system works and if the AG and feds choose to do nothing with that information—for example, if they've been bought off—the *Tribune* and other news outlets will get a real prize: a detailed report of your shenanigans with Carlton."

Rusco was now listening with quiet dread.

"Oh, that's right, you didn't know Carlton kept a diary containing his sick narrative about all the illegal shit he ever did. I found it in his library a year and a half ago, and guess what? —You star in a lot of it: details with dates, names, what happened and where, and the money that was involved. Unfortunately, there was nothing about the Panama accounts in it or we'd have had this discussion a long time ago."

She looked hard at him, "There's enough there to put you in prison for life…or on death row. But don't worry," she paused, "the diary's in a safe place as long as you don't do anything foolish."

Rusco was stunned and, for a moment, couldn't think of his next move. He sputtered, "I don't know what to say…you've learned a lot from someone, and you've insinuated some awful things about me. Who have you been talking to? To whom do I owe the thanks for this information download?" Then he realized, *Given the timing of this, if information regarding the accounts hadn't been in the diary, she must have learned about them from Damen during their meeting last week.*

Anita knew she had him by the short hairs and said in a firm voice, "That's none of your business, Gene. The important thing is that we work together from now on to take advantage of those accounts and the estate that Carlton left behind. After all, you *are* the executor." She stood up and ended the meeting after telling him she was going to relinquish the insurance claim.

"Arthur," she called—he'd been waiting in the hall and entered the room—"Mr. Rusco is leaving. Please escort him out." She continued, "Gene, please try to be here Saturday morning so we can talk after I meet with Dr. Damen."

Rusco was dumbfounded and wobbled out of the room. He drove to his office and called Panama to confirm what she told him. It was true: she'd completed the paperwork for her shares of the accounts, and he'd lost over thirty million dollars. Gone.

He had never been so dominated by a woman and kicked himself for underestimating her. *She's damn smart*, he thought, *and underneath that beguiling demeanor is one tough and cunning bitch.* In all the meetings they'd had since Carlton died, she never let on that she knew anything about the shady and illegal things he'd done with him. Recalling what just happened and the prurient stories Carlton told him about her, he got an erection that quickly left, a casualty of his deflated ego.

That half of the money in the accounts was still his soothed the shock and humiliation he felt, but only two days had passed and the son-of-a-bitch responsible for everything was standing in front of him.

Rusco did not shake Damen's outstretched hand. Damen ignored the insult and said, "Good morning, Gene." He hoped today would be the last time he'd see him.

Anita's manservant, Arthur, was behind Rusco and saw their exchange. He stepped forward and motioned inside. "Good morning, Dr. Damen. Mrs. Solishe is waiting for you. Shall we?"

"Good morning, Arthur. Yes, thank you."

They walked to the parlor where Damen and Anita had met before. She was seated in a red leather chair, stood up smiling, and offered a firm, ice-cold handshake. Rusco, who had trailed behind Arthur and Damen, left the room without saying a word.

Anita said, "Good morning, Dr. Damen. Thank you for coming today." She pointed to a dark green and maroon sofa. "Have a seat. Arthur, please pour us some coffee." Looking at Damen, she said, "Dr., we have a superb Costa Rican blend and some delicious biscotti."

Damen said, "Thank you. It looks wonderful."

Arthur served the coffee and biscotti, and closed the door as he exited.

"Dr. Damen, I'd like to get directly to why we're meeting today."

"Thank you. I was hoping we'd do that."

"Coping with Carlton's death has been difficult for me, and this entire process with the insurance company is frustrating beyond belief. I'm not blaming you. In fact, I'm thankful for your candor and the information you provided during our last meeting about the Panama accounts—as you probably know, I've already made sure I can access my share of the money. The rest of what you told me, though, your theory about how Carlton died, is *rubbish*—that Rahel, Julia, and I conspired to avenge our father's death? Medication patches? Honey? Jewish Brigade?—absolute garbage, and I'll deny all of it until the day I die. And if your so-called evidence is as solid as you said, you should go to the police and let this play out in court, but I don't think you'll do that because when the jury says, "Not guilty," the company *you're* working for, Brantel, will be *required* to give me the twenty-million dollars from Carlton's life insurance policy."

Damen sat quietly and watched her. He knew she was being prudent and saying this for documentation of her claims of innocence should testimony under oath in future legal proceedings about this discussion be necessary.

"And you've come up with an alternative, a plan where it's guaranteed the insurance company won't have to shell out a nickel, a trial won't be needed, and I get over thirty million dollars tax-free from the Panama accounts. Let me tell you something, ordinarily I'd play everything by the book and let the truth speak for itself in our judicial system, but this deal's too good for me to pass up, and besides, no one's harmed by it," she said self-righteously.

What an actress, he thought, *with a calculated, well-delivered performance.*

"So, Dr. Damen, I've told you I'm innocent, but how can you convince me you won't turn your so-called evidence and the other information you've gathered over to the authorities as soon as I relinquish my claim to Carlton's insurance policy? I'd be out twenty million dollars and possibly have to undergo the trauma of a trial, and who knows what might happen with money in the Panama accounts?"

"Mrs. Solishe, I know everything there's to know about you: your family's history, the details of your life from childhood onward, your likes, dislikes, and pleasures, the choices you've made. I haven't walked in your shoes and can't judge what you've done—that's way above my pay grade. What I do know is that you're not an evil person.

"Evil people harm others for self-gratification—financial, sexual, social, psychological—and they do it without regret and more than once. Mr. Solishe was evil, cruel, insensitive, and vindictive, and he died as a result. I have proof he was killed—you deny doing it—but what would be gained by me turning you in?

"We talked about a trial, which would be long and brutal. You, your sisters, and others would be tarnished and might end up in prison, and your children would be socially tattooed forever, perhaps without family for years, all because an evil man got his just desserts.

"I believe you and I are a lot alike: when an evil act is done to us, we take it personally and respond in kind toward whoever harmed us or those we love. We take revenge, and that's bad, but unlike Carlton we have consciences and carry the emotional baggage from our actions into the future.

"In my profession and personal life I've had to deal with people who are evil. The precepts of my profession mandate I try to preserve the life and health of my patients regardless of their moral compasses or behaviors, and I've been true to that code. Faith and dedication to my God guide decisions in my personal life, and I'm ashamed to say I've had shortcomings there that will haunt me forever.

"Had I dealt with Mr. Solishe in the way you and the others did, I'd feel good in the short run but suffer later. A trial and probable incarceration would be painful, but it could provide closure for you and the others, a sense of debt to society paid through punishment served. By letting you go free, I'm not doing you a favor because guilt from killing Carlton will fester and torture your consciences—I know this."

Anita said, "It might, *if* I did what you've asserted. As it is, I loved Carlton to the end and *did not kill him*, so you can spare the sanctimony—I don't need your psychoanalysis and moralizing. Don't get me wrong, I like the option you've come up with because I'll be compensated fairly without a lot of negative publicity or legal and insurance garbage." She paused, "However, I have questions that require answers before I sign away my insurance rights."

The meeting went on for ninety minutes. Afterwards, Damen emerged from the parlor with Anita Solishe's signature disavowing any claim to Carlton Solishe's twenty-million-dollar life insurance policy.

Rusco appeared out of nowhere as Anita accompanied Damen through the foyer toward the front door. He hated Damen's guts—over thirty-two million dollars lost, half the money in the Panama accounts plus the money Anita promised him from the insurance settlement because of his meddling.

They walked to the front porch where Anita concluded her discussion with Damen, performing again, but this time for Rusco's benefit.

"As I told you, Dr. Damen, I was devastated by Carlton's death, and the investigation by your insurance company has forced me to relive it. I've gotten to where I can't sleep at night, I'm not eating, and I've lost a lot of weight. After you mentioned the possibility of a trial and exhuming poor Carlton's corpse, I started seeing a psychiatrist to help with my emotions. I don't need the twenty million dollars and, like I explained, it's just not worth it... I'm not sure I could survive what that would entail. Carlton wasn't an easy man to live with, and as you and your investigators learned, he did some pretty rotten things over the years. Nonetheless, I loved him... Some men deserve to die, Dr. Damen, and I'm sure there are people who feel Carlton was one of those, but not me. Like we talked about, I didn't have anything to do with his death—besides, only God or a jury should make that kind of judgement."

Her words struck a raw chord in Damen's soul because they reminded him of times in the past when he'd acted as God, as judge, jury, and executioner, and his tight mental reins began to fray under the weight of guilt from his moral missteps during this investigation. He was tired, and his muscles and heart quivered...it was time to leave and get back to Emmi and the river.

"I understand." He shook Anita's hand. "Goodbye, Mrs. Solishe."

She said, "Goodbye, Dr. Damen," and turned to go inside.

As Damen stepped down the first step, Rusco threatened under his breath, "Spend your consulting fee quickly, Dr. Damen. I won't forget what you did here."

Damen stopped and opened his briefcase. "That reminds me, Gene, this was left at my hotel and is addressed to you." He handed over the manila envelope and lied, "I don't know who it's from," and walked to his car.

Puzzled, Rusco opened the envelope. He pulled out a glossy picture, then staggered back against the doorframe, ashen in terror. Jimmy Kelly's nude and mutilated body looked up through the bloody message, "You're *next*."

Damen drove away without looking back.

CHAPTER 23 – HELP NEEDED

Penelope Liu was dreaming that she was in Stockholm receiving the Nobel Prize in Medicine from the King of Sweden for her pediatric research at Palo Alto when her private-line cell phone rang. A sleepy glance at the dressing table clock revealed it was 11 p.m. She rolled in bed and picked up the flashing dream-slayer, expecting the worst because no one called the president of Southern University at this time on a Sunday night unless there was a major problem.

"Hello, this is Penelope Liu."

There was silence…then a deep leaden voice she hardly recognized.

"Dr. Liu, this is Jack Damen, and I need your help."

Silence.

Liu said, "Jack? Are you there?"

"Yeah. Sorry…the good news is the Brantel Mutual investigation into the death of their policy-holder is just about over and Stuart Castelman won't lose a nickel. The bad news is my PTSD is running wild again and I've got to get down to the river. Otherwise, by tomorrow I'll be a basket case and in the psych ward. I need someone to take over my Team 2 hospital service responsibilities in the morning, and to oversee my research lab. I'm not sure when I'll be back—"

She said without delay, "Jack, I'll get it done. Are you sure you're OK to drive down there? I can arrange for a student worker to take you down."

Damen slurred, "I've got a cab to take me. It's a long drive, but what the hell? Besides, I don't want anybody at Southern seeing me right now."

Liu's heart sank. *He's been drinking*, she concluded, *and who knows what will happen next. I shouldn't have asked him to do this. Sure, Castelman will be happy, but I put this man in an awful position: respond to my request or turn it down and risk making me mad, his boss, and lose a lot of money for the scholarship fund dedicated to Beth, his life's love. I'm such a shit sometimes…but it goes with being president of this place.*

"Jack, I appreciate what you've done. Be careful."

Damen said, "Thanks for taking care of things," and hung up.

Liu got out of bed, went into her home office, and pulled up a directory of faculty private phone numbers. It was 1:00 a.m. before she completed her final call. *There will be a lot of unhappy faculty because of reshuffled schedules and responsibilities*, she thought, *but I'll make it up to them by acknowledging their dedication at the annual faculty award ceremony and providing written commendations for their academic portfolios. It's just another part of the job...* She went back to sleep anticipating Stuart would fill her in tomorrow about what caused Damen's breakdown, not realizing there were lingering questions about the investigation and its conclusions and it would be over two weeks before Castelman could meet with Damen to talk about them. And that afterwards, there'd be aspects about Carlton Solishe's death he'd never understand.

Damen made another call that night. The phone rang several times before a sleepy voice answered.

"Yeah?"

"Joon, this Jack Damen."

Lee perked up. Damen's voice was different—deeper, with sadness, and gurgling in his throat.

"Hey, Dr. Damen. What's going on?"

Damen said, "I'm not going to be back with the team tomorrow morning. The investigation I've been working on, the one y'all know about, has wiped me out and I need some time off." He sniffled, swallowed, and cleared his throat. "Dr. Liu is arranging coverage for me. Please tell the rest of the team I'll be back as soon as I can and that I'll miss them." His voice darkened with immeasurable despair, "Goodbye," and he hung up.

Lee thought, *Fuck...*

CHAPTER 24 – AFTER THE CRASH: BLACK, WHITE, AND GRAY

As with his previous spells, Emmi was there for Damen when he got down to the river —he hadn't told her he was coming, but when they talked by phone a few days ago, he let her know the investigation had gotten complicated and was troubling him. She moved in and cared for him 24/7, and between her and the soothing river, his soul once again pulled itself together. In three weeks, he was back at home in the City of Medicine. Before returning to work at Southern Medical Center, however, he needed a psychiatric evaluation: University President Dr. Liu had required it. That was done yesterday, and he was cleared for usual job responsibilities —rounds, teaching, research—and to meet with Stuart Castelman, CEO of Brantel Mutual, whose intuition about Carlton Solishe's death led to Damen's involvement in the investigation, for a wrap-up session. He looked forward to teaching Team 2 again but not to answering questions Castelman might have regarding his dealings with Anita Solishe or the vitreous sample he'd sent to Brantel's team for analysis .

The team surprised Damen when he walked into the hospital classroom for morning rounds. After learning when he would be back, they plotted a mini-celebration with balloons, streamers, Cream Delight doughnuts, hot coffee, and a "Welcome Back Dr. D" sign on the wall. As soon as he entered, they sang an improvised, "Nice To Have You Back" jingle, and he got handshakes and shoulder bumps from Joon, Mark, and Nyquim, and hugs from Julie, Michelle (whose long and snug hug surprised him), and Holly.

He teared up and said, "You don't know how much this means to me. The insurance case was more than I could handle, and I had a breakdown, pure and simple. I mean, I suffered during the investigation, but so did you with me being preoccupied and gone at times, particularly over the past few weeks. Thank you...thank you, for your support and understanding; you've hung in there and are such kind and caring people." He wiped his wet cheeks with his fingers. "It's more than I deserve."

Damen's emotions caught them off-guard. A straightforward man, he had always been empathetic and compassionate toward their patients but without exaggerated emotions, the stable ship in any medical storm. Now he was thinner, his smiles weren't as wide, and he seemed vulnerable. In one of those "Ah-ha" moments, they realized he loved them, and that his teams and students fill the void in his heart from losing Beth, the woman he cherished and about whom they'd heard the rumors swirling at Southern. They were his children, and he a surrogate father, there to protect and guide them through the jungles of medicine and self-discovery.

There wasn't a dry eye in the room. The team had gone through a lot over the last several months caring for sick and dying patients and learning they could have done better. They'd had to confront their professional and personal shortcomings without illusions, face the essence of who they are, and choose through their actions who they wanted to be. Damen showed them this process never ends, in life or in medicine, and they had coalesced into a team that relished the thought of working together again.

They finished their doughnuts and walked to 5 North.

Southern Medical Center was bustling. Its beds were full, and doctors, nurses, and support staff were operating at full tilt. That didn't prevent Adele Sharpson, R.N., Charge Nurse on 5 North, from breaking away from her computer and hugging Damen. She'd seen him after other bad times, and she said, "Welcome back Jack. We've all missed you."

Damen tightened his face and eyes to keep back the emotional bubble in his chest and knew he was where he belonged: caring for sick patients and teaching others to do the same. *It's the only way for me to go forward*, Damen thought—*to help the sick, keep my personal demons at bay, and support the things and people I love*. An image of Beth…poor Beth…came through strong and he closed his eyes for a minute to keep his composure.

Sharpson said, "You okay?"

He hesitated and gave her a small smile. "Yeah. Thanks, Adele. This one's going to take some time."

She looked at him. He'd lost weight he didn't need to lose. The doctors at Southern were very smart, especially Damen, but they had the same personal struggles as everyone else and sometimes worse with all their responsibilities. It wouldn't be needed but, just in case, she'd keep a close eye on things for a while and have his back; he'd done it many times for her and the other nurses on this floor. She gave him a squeeze, whispered, "You're the best," and went back to her station.

The Team dove into rounds. Everything went well. There were no major patient-care disagreements or disasters and they were done by early afternoon. Afterwards, Damen met with Stuart Castelman in one of the small conference rooms off the main cafeteria to discuss the Carlton Solishe case.

Castelman stood up and greeted him. "Jack, it's good seeing you. You're looking well," he lied. Damen had lost a lot of weight and his face was thinner than the last time they'd met.

Damen nodded and said, "You too, Stuart."

They sat down.

"Jack, really nice work on the case... You don't know how surprised I was when you called and sent me Anita Solishe's policy disclaimer. Unbelievable. It saved us a whole bunch of money and you'll be getting a ten percent reward, about two million dollars."

Damen said, "Thanks, but I can't accept it because of the University laws against 'double dipping.' You could make out a check to Southern and give it to Dr. Liu, though. There are some wonderful educational funds that help students lower their medical school debts, and we made a deal when I agreed to do this that allows me to designate some of the money to those or a research fund."

"Great, we'll do that," concurred Castelman.

He continued. "Jack, there are a couple of things I need to talk with you about. I read our investigative team's final report, and this case involved issues and people way beyond Carlton and Anita Solishe. I didn't know about your military background or connections with the Cirazzis and the Mob—the team stumbled onto it while looking into some loose ends in the case—but they seem to have been in play during this investigation. I'd like you to share with me whatever you feel comfortable with."

Stumbled onto it? My ass, thought Damen. *They checked me out just like they snooped into everyone involved with Carlton's death.*

Castelman felt a chill go up his back as Damen's eyes went from the warmth of a friendly German Shepard to the cold darkness of an alpha timber wolf.

Damen said with warning, "Stuart, you asked me to look into Carlton Solishe's death and save Brantel some money if possible. I did that—you won't have to pay out a cent beyond the investigation expenses—and I'm glad I could help. But as you know, it was hard on me and I had to take some time off afterward. I'm not reliving it. I'll talk about my report and what I discovered, but I won't discuss my personal life or any friends or acquaintances."

"OK..., I'm OK with that." Castelman hadn't expected this response and degree of reticence and wondered immediately about what had really happened in Chicago.

"Also," Damen continued, "I'll need your word that you won't share any information you've learned during this investigation with *anyone*. Otherwise, this discussion is over."

Castelman said, "Jack, you know that as CEO of Brantel I have to report anything that's illegal to the authorities."

Damon stood up. "Thanks for asking me to help. Just send the check to Dr. Liu."

"Wait... Jack, this isn't the first time something like this has transpired. We uncover a lot of things during these kinds of investigations and some of it is pretty outrageous...and illegal. To be honest, we don't report it unless required to by law or there's danger to innocents. I don't have any trouble keeping what you say between us as long as I or any Brantel employee can't be held liable."

Damen resumed his seat and brusquely said, "Okay. What questions do you have?"

Castelman said, "I don't have any questions—it's just there are problems with your final report. To be blunt, based on a review of your findings, our investigators don't believe your conclusions are correct. So, I'd like to summarize what you wrote to make sure I understand what you were thinking."

Damen frowned, and fidgeted in his chair. "Sure,

go ahead."

"You believe Anita got clonidine transdermal patches from Rahel who had been using the medication for hypertension. She put them on Carlton's back when he was asleep from the lorazepam, ran Turkish honey into his feeding tube, and killed him by slowing down his heart rate. And that's why you got the postmortem vitreous sample from his eyes and sent it to us for clonidine analysis.

Castelman continued. "And her motive was that Carlton drove her father, Istvan, to suicide. She discovered this after reading Carlton's diary, *Cervantes*, which she happened upon in his library. After learning how and why Istvan was targeted —pure revenge intended to hurt her—she shared everything with Rahel and Julia. So they killed him and embroidered insignias of the World War II Jewish Brigade to go under Istvan's pictures at their homes in celebration of their vengeance... So far, so good?"

"Yeah."

"You told Anita you had proof of their crime and they'd go to prison or, at minimum, be publicly humiliated by salacious information from their trials. To avoid this, you offered her a better option: forego arrest and a trial, no negative publicity, and still come out thirty million dollars ahead. All she had to do was sign a disclaimer to Carlton's insurance; you took care of the rest. Because she knew you were right about the clonidine, the honey, and the embroidered insignias, she cooperated to save herself and her sisters from prosecution."

"Right. That's about it. So, what's the problem, Stuart?"

Castelman said, "Jack, the clonidine analysis on the vitreous was *negative!*"

Feigning surprise, Damen jerked up in his chair, eyes and mouth open. "What? It couldn't be—"

"Nope, no clonidine there. *None.* So, your theory about why she disclaimed her right to the policy payout doesn't hold water." Castelman hesitated. "The question is, why did she do it and give up twenty million dollars?"

Damon seemed distracted and appeared to be going back through his thoughts. "I don't know... unless I completely misjudged her. She said she wouldn't be able to take the strain if Carleton was exhumed. Maybe she was telling the truth. She denied reading his diary, and if she didn't believe he drove her father to suicide and hated him as much as I thought, maybe getting thirty million dollars from the Panama accounts and avoiding the emotional pain of him being dug up was what did it. Damn! Could she have still loved him after all he had put her through?"

Castelman said, "That's what we think. It's fortunate that Carleton and Rusco set up those Panamanian accounts. Otherwise, we'd be paying twenty million dollars to her: given the absence of clonidine in the vitreous, there's insufficient evidence to prove Carlton died of anything except natural causes. We believe your theory about the honey is far-fetched—there was no mention in the autopsy report of unusual stomach contents, and the toxicology report was negative on what was there. There are no tests specific for that type of honey, but we believe if he was given enough to kill him with the additive effects of clonidine, excessive residue would have been found in the stomach. As far as the embroidered insignias under Istvan's pictures are concerned, a more plausible explanation is they were put there in remembrance of the family's relatives killed by the Nazis during the Holocaust and the revenge dealt out by members of the Jewish Brigade after the war. Our investigators felt your assertion that the insignias were symbols of a successful conspiracy by the sisters to kill Carlton had no supporting evidence—and I'm sorry to say this—it just didn't seem realistic."

Concealing his true emotions, Damen had wilted in his chair and looked at the floor. Raising his eyes and slowly shaking his head, he said, "Whew, I haven't been this wrong in years." *This is perfect*, he thought, *perfect...*

"Jack, don't feel bad. Most of this is conjecture. What we know for sure is that clonidine wasn't in the vitreous sample. Without that or other firm evidence pointing to foul play, Anita was entitled to the insurance settlement. She still loved that bum. Enough so that whatever you told her about exhumation sank in and she chose to give up her rights to Carlton's policy and take the thirty million dollars plus in the Panama accounts rather than claim the insurance in addition to the money in the accounts and suffer the emotional toll of reliving Carlton's death during a lengthy trial. Twenty million dollars is a lot of money to give up, so she must have really loved him, as hard as that is to believe."

"I guess you are right, Stuart… I'm still amazed."

Castelman said, "The important thing is you did a great job for us. We'd never have investigated Rusco and some of the areas involving her friends, neighbors, and sisters without your requests. Or Kelly. And you used the information about the Panama accounts and the specter of Carlton's exhumation to guide her away from claiming his policy. I'm convinced your experience as a doctor was key in establishing a good relationship with her and, even though your conclusions were off-base, you saved Brantel twenty million dollars."

"Thanks. There's a good side to me being wrong, though, isn't there? If the clonidine test had been positive, you'd need to turn the sisters in to the police despite their good deed for humanity. As it is, you and Brantel Mutual are off the moral hook—no hard evidence of a crime, just the suspicions of a crazed investigating doctor. Seems like a win-win for everyone: insurance company gets to keep its money and a human piece of crap leaves the earth. Personally, I'd have let her go regardless of the results from the vitreous sample."

Castelman squirmed in his chair and stared at Damen. He believed in the rule of law and looked up to physicians as moral and ethical stalwarts. But here was the physician he respected more than any other saying that if Anita and her sisters had killed Carlton, it would be okay for them to walk free. This ran counter to everything Castelman believed and, in a self-righteous side thought, he wished the vitreous sample had been positive so he could put her behind bars.

He said with conviction, "Jack, I don't agree with you. If the vitreous had been positive, we'd turn the whole thing over to the authorities and Anita and whoever helped her would have to face the consequences."

Damen tightened his lips. "We'll agree to disagree this round, won't we? Are we about done?"

"I think so… At least I didn't ask you about Kelly or any of those matters."

"Yes, that was good," Damen said with a strained smile. "I should be getting back upstairs to our patients."

"Jack, thanks again. I'll call if we have any other questions." Castelman paused. "And we'll get the check to Dr. Liu as soon as possible."

"Thanks, I appreciate it."

They shook hands and Damen left the room.

Castelman sat alone for a while thinking about the investigation. It was as complicated as any Brantel had had during the eight years he'd been CEO. Without clonidine in the vitreous, there were evidentiary loose ends suggesting foul play, but they were circumstantial and could have lawful explanations. So, no crimes were committed except the theft and money laundering of millions from SCI by Carlton and Rusco. SCI never missed the money and their investors got above-market returns anyway thanks to Carlton's investment genius. And the accounting firm that performed its annual audits covered up any irregularities in the books. Perfect, no need to act there.

Then, there's Damen, he mused. *He's clear from a legal perspective because he isn't obligated to notify the U.S. Department of Justice about the accounts, and he won't personally benefit from the reward being given to Southern. What an odd duck, though. He's the best doctor in one of the best medical schools in the country, but he's haunted by a violent and tragic past.* Brantel's investigative team had been able to access records about Damen's military service in Columbia, and their final report provided a good assessment of what had happened in San Francisco and how the Mob and its high-priced lawyer helped him and Beth out. Castelman didn't believe in coincidence and thought about how Kelly suddenly vanished after DNA analysis had linked him to the murder of an Italian woman thirty years ago in Rochester; Damen had been the last person at the Solishe estate to see him.

Connecting the dots painted the picture of a different Jack Damen than anyone at Southern had seen. Castelman wondered how much Penelope knew about him; probably little beyond his academic work. Brantel's corporate policies prevented disclosures about findings from their investigations, so he'd have to be careful not to say anything inappropriate to her about him.

Castelman took a deep breath, pulled himself out of his reverie, put on his CEO hat, and relaxed. The investigation couldn't have turned out better, he concluded—Carlton Solishe had a natural death, *but* there was no huge policy payout. Outstanding! And, Damen might be useful in future cases, albeit less stressful ones.

Three floors above, Damen was climbing the stairwell to 5 North. *I'm so glad*, he smiled, *that Mrs. Gre-*

umach's dog hadn't eaten a box of clonidine patches before it died chasing a car. Muffy had such large eyes.

And only Jasper and I know the whole story...

CHAPTER 25 – WHAT JASPER KNOWS

The night before Damen returned to work and met with Stuart Castelman, he sat in the dark red leather recliner in his den and watched flames flicker in the fireplace. It was a year-round indulgence for him irrespective of seasonal weather. A sweet-smelling, warm coffee vapor rose from Jasper's head and filled the room, another treat despite the eighty-degree heat outside.

He wanted to be well-rested for tomorrow—back with the team after almost three weeks away, hospital rounds into the afternoon and for the meeting with Castelman—but he needed to dialogue with Jasper before going to bed. Talking to the big-eyed, ceramic face mug after solving a difficult medical problem had been a ritual for many years: he reviewed the case, examined his decision-making, and determined how he could have done better. And, he recorded it for review one month later to detect missed nuances that would have changed his approach to the case. The process had been invaluable to him for learning, and following this investigation, he knew it would be paramount for self-healing. Certain facts and actions he had taken were too hazardous for him to transcribe, however, because it was general knowledge at Southern that he did this and there was a small chance this recording might be subpoenaed in future legal proceedings. *No worry,* Damen winced, *I'll never be able to forget those things anyhow...*

He switched on the recorder.

"Jasper, we meet again, and what a joy," he said with sarcasm. "Case solved, diagnoses confirmed, and mission accomplished! Except this time, the rot in brilliant Dr. Damen's soul has resurfaced with immoral, unethical, and illegal decisions to save a fat-cat insurance company some bucks. I worked out an arrangement where Carlton's murderers could avoid prosecution and collaborated with Brantel's investigators to snoop, legally and illegally, into the most private areas of people's lives —*and turned a killer over to the mob for retribution*, he thought—what a good person I am! Such fine examples of civic responsibility! So much for my illusions about who I've become... That and the briar patch of memories about Beth's ordeal in San Francisco precipitated the worst breakdown I've had since leaving the Rangers. Shit, at one point I thought about swallowing a bullet. But every day I was recovering at the river, Emmi reminded me about my obligation to Beth and forced me to look beyond this mess and focus on making my dark side better."

The psychopathology had been awful and he still didn't know how he got through it: Carlton, Kelly, and Rusco were messed up, and Anita and the others weren't saints either. But Carlton was the worst by far, a heinous, wretched person who embodied a Hopkins professor's adage, "The more you meet people, the more you like cancer."

Damen continued, "Brantel's investigative team must have spent a million dollars traveling, bribing people, and breaking into databases and private properties to learn everything about him. Where facts were lacking, there were enough incidental dots to complete the picture of Carlton's life. And his death. The team was like the FBI but without guidelines and restrictions, and I was able to figure out that Anita killed him with the help of her sisters, why they did it, and how it was done.

"Finding the motive was key. The man treated Anita and everyone else like shit, molested his children and the son of a close family friend, and got sexual kicks by psychologically destroying people. But he did this over many years and no one had killed him. Something changed and, because he'd been bedbound and incapacitated for five years, it had to be something in the past that surfaced and enraged Anita and her sisters. Brantel's investigators talking with the prostitutes in Thailand and buying a copy of his diary from their pimps revealed it: Carlton had written down the details of how he drove Istvan to suicide and reveled about hiding the diary in his home library, "Where my dumb shit wife will never find it." But she did, and it cost him his life.

"With his financial background, Carlton knew the psychological importance of financial independence to retirees; he also knew that many choose to kill themselves when their nest eggs are depleted. So, he hired Andrew Dillon, the private investigator, to look into Istvan's retirement finances and lifestyle. Dillon found that Istvan was living on limited income from a separation buyout by the tool and die company where he had worked for twenty years, plus social security. His house was paid off and he got by without financial assistance from his children. But he was lonely. Anita's mother, Rebeka, died several years before, so Istvan sought company twice a week in a small neighborhood bar where he talked with people over the one beer he could afford each evening.

"It was easy for Carlton to devise a plot that would lead to Istvan's death. It was set in motion after Gene Rusco found two crooks who'd emigrated from Hungary and wanted to go back. Over several months, they befriended Istvan at the bar by telling tales about the homeland and treating him to drinks and food from their cash-thick wallets. They drove a BMW 7-series sedan and claimed to be venture capitalists—in Istvan's eyes, they had realized 'the American dream.' Eager to improve his situation, he invested his retirement nest egg in a factitious real estate development project; once the money left his bank account, he never saw it or them again.

"He went to the Chicago authorities, but the understaffed police department had higher priorities than investigating bad decisions by an aged retiree who'd been conned. Later, as part of Brantel's investigation, the bar's surveillance videos were analyzed and Istvan's 'investment friends' matched airport security photos of passengers on a subsequent flight to Budapest. Knowing their identities enabled Brantel to trace his money, plus matching funds from Carlton, to their Hungarian bank. They weren't arrested because the amount stolen was insufficient to justify international prosecution.

"Too proud to admit to his children that he had been swindled, and unaware his son-in-law had orchestrated the scam, Istvan realized he'd have to ask his children for financial support for routine living expenses; this was unacceptable, so he hung himself. Julia went to his house three days later after he didn't return her calls and found him in the garage.

"Carlton felt it was one of his great accomplishments. He described in *Cervantes* how he organized everything, how Anita came to him crying about Istvan's death, how he reassured her regarding her importance in his life, and how he exploited her emotional vulnerability with frequent demands for sex. He wrote how they cried together, she from grief, and him from masked laughter and delight. And he underlined, 'I finally got the bitch and I'm SO happy.'

"Anita read all of this and shared it with Rahel and Julia. I realized Rahel knew about the diary when she slipped-up and said with certainty that Carlton killed her father. Recognizing the mistake, she tried to backtrack and concocted a flimsy explanation for her strong feelings. The story fell apart when she said Anita felt Carlton treated Istvan well: Carlton didn't treat anyone well. And Julia, she had to have known about the diary—there was no other explanation for the hatred she exuded toward Carlton when I interviewed her. The clinchers indicating their involvement were multiple visits to the Solishe estate during Carlton's final weeks and the embroidered insignias of the Jewish Brigade beneath their father's picture in their homes, triumphant reminders of the vengeful roles they played with Anita.

"The daughters were furious about what Carlton had done to Istvan and wanted him brought to justice. However, they were realistic regarding a judicial outcome: given his status—bedbound, mentally compromised, and unable to effectively communicate—he would never be punished to their satisfaction. So they decided to kill him, and with her pharmacy background, Anita was the ideal bandleader. She coordinated the steps perfectly... Well, almost perfectly.

"Her slip-up was she didn't know clonidine levels in the vitreous of a dead person's eyes remain elevated for several days after death and can be measured later if a sample is taken at autopsy." Damen turned off the recorder and continued talking. "The Lake County Coroner, Dr. Daniel Lange, sent me a sample of Carlton's vitreous and I had it analyzed by our forensic laboratory at Southern. It was positive for clonidine, and bingo, my suspicions were confirmed.

"So there it was: motive and methods."

He turned the recorder back on.

"What I had to do was convince Anita she might go to prison and that there was a safer way for her to get a lot of money than claiming the insurance. It was an unconventional proposal for me to make, for sure, and the first conversation we had alone at the Solishe estate about it deteriorated in a hurry when I accused her of conspiring with Rahel and Julia to kill Carlton."

" . . . Your family's the most important thing in life for you, and while you couldn't prove he molested your children, you read his account of how he took pleasure in destroying your dad to hurt you. So you and your sisters decided to kill him."

Anita's stare hardened.

Damen said, "How you did it was ingenious and a testimony to your pharmacy training. You'd have known large amounts of clonidine can lower a person's heart rate to a fatal level, but what stumped me were the autopsy pictures of Mr. Solishe's skin where you attached Rahel's clonidine skin patches—I've seen those skin changes in my patients using clonidine patches—because he might have survived the small number of patches you put on him.

"Although he took diltiazem to control his heart rate from atrial fibrillation, a large number of patches would have been needed to slow his heart rate to a fatal level. But because the patches had to be put on hairless areas to avoid telltale residue on hairs, you were limited in the number you could put on his back; and they needed to be on his back because skin discolorations there could be attributed to mattress pressure whereas markings elsewhere on his body would be suspicious. So you came up with an additional way to lower his heart rate further: mad honey.

"It was brilliant, truly! You and Mr. Solishe used Turkish honey from the nectar of Rhododendron ponticum as an aphrodisiac for years. I suspect you discovered its sexual use from researching the Nazis at the Holocaust Museum or reading about Rhododendrons at the Botanic Garden. You knew it can slow down the heart, and you learned how to adjust the amounts used to maximize sexual enjoyment and minimize the risk. When you, Rahel, and Julia decided to kill Carlton, the tools were at hand: his usual diltiazem, Rahel's clonidine, and the mad honey. Because medication side effects are additive, combining them in sufficient amounts would be fatal."

Anita gasped and feigned astonishment. "Rahel? Julia? Mad honey? What are you talking about?"

"Come on, Rahel's clonidine is a no-brainer. Her blood pressure was stable on clonidine for many years, then started going up when she skipped doses to give you the patches. Before he added another medication to lower the pressure, her physician wrote in his office notes that he suspected she wasn't taking her medication. And, her pressure returned to normal after Mr. Solishe died even though she stopped getting refills of the second medication; it's obvious she began taking the clonidine again.

"Regarding Julia, visitor logs from the guardhouse

show she and Rahel visited four times in the two weeks before Mr. Solishe died. They'd only visited once in the previous three years. A harmless coincidence?...I don't think so, and neither would a jury. And of course, there were the embroidered insignias of the World War II Jewish Brigade underneath the pictures of your dad, Istvan, in each of their homes."

Damen saw Anita's eyes widen in surprise for a second, then narrow.

"And wherever you keep your family pictures here, I'm sure Istvan's picture is sitting on one. The Brigade fought in the Italian Campaign in 1945, and right after the war, some of its members formed a group, Tilhas Tizig Gesheften, that conducted revenge assassinations on former Nazis. The three of you couldn't mount Carlton's head as a trophy, so one of you embroidered the insignias to serve as daily reminders that you had killed him and avenged Istvan's death—"

Her face tightened and she bared her teeth, "How dare you say something like that! You're crazy!"

He softened his voice. "Please, Mrs. Solishe, let me go on. I stumbled upon the mad honey during my interview with Mary Hollender. Close friends share secrets and, based on how much we discovered they buy, Mary and Chet Hollender must enjoy the honey a lot. Mary served it to me on biscuits that day; she said she found the combination 'invigorating.' When we walked out through her kitchen, sitting on the counter was an open jar, and always looking for tasty, 'feel good' foods, I researched the brand afterwards and discovered its non-gustatory uses. Otherwise, I wouldn't have known about it."

Anita paled.

"The evening before he died, you gave him his lorazepam as usual and he went to sleep. Afterwards, you ran the mad honey into his feeding tube and waited several hours for it to have its full effect and move through his stomach so it wouldn't be seen at autopsy. Then you stuck the clonidine patches on his back. Sometime after that his heart rate bottomed out and he died. All you had to do was get up early, take off the patches, and remove any adhesive residue."

She raged, "Get out of my house! I've heard enough of your fantasies, and I shouldn't have talked with you without my lawyer being here."

"Mrs. Solishe, you misunderstand my motives here. I don't care how Mr. Solishe died or that you had something to do with it. My only interest is saving Brantel Mutual twenty million dollars—"

She interrupted him. "That's obvious. Now get out!"

Damen put his hand up in surrender. "Mrs. Solishe, please listen to me. I have proof that Mr.

Solishe was given clonidine before he died...*proof!* After exhumation of Mr. Solishe's body and a long and sensational trial, you'll never get the money and every detail about Mr. Solishe and you will become public knowledge. Your sisters, children, and friends—like the Hollenders—will be dragged through the mud. And there's a good chance you, Rahel, and Julia will end up in prison; maybe Mary Hollender too.

Anita frowned with disbelief, "Proof?"

"Yeah, proof! But there's a way to avoid all of this: no exhumation, no trial, no muckraking. And, you'll end up with more money."

"Hold on. First, you accuse me of murder, then speculate how I did it. You tell me Carlton will be exhumed, everyone's lives will be exposed and destroyed, and I'll end up in prison. Now you want to help me? What the hell is going on?"

Damen's eyes became emotionless, and Anita felt a chill. He said, "I know you loved him early in the marriage, but Mr. Solishe was an evil and cruel man. In my opinion, he got what he deserved, just not soon enough. He wrecked a lot of lives and it doesn't seem right that more should be destroyed after he's gone." Damen paused. "If there's any truth in what I've told you, please believe what I'm about to say."

Anita hesitated. "Dr. Damen, your theory about

Carlton's death is a bunch of crap, and I *did not* kill him." She tightened her face and stared at Damen. "However, I'd be a fool not to listen how I might avoid being tormented through a trial and Carlton's exhumation and still come out ahead financially."

Damen said, "OK, but there's over thirty million dollars involved here. If you get greedy and try to claim the insurance policy money in addition to this money, I'll turn over what I have to the authorities and you'll never have a chance to spend any of it."

"Yeah, yeah. I said I didn't kill him, but go ahead and tell me what you're thinking."

"So Jasper, I told her about the accounts in Panama and the legal statute that made half of the money hers. I gave her the phone numbers where she could make her claims. All she had to do was call, fax the necessary paperwork with Carlton's death certificate, and the money would be hers.

"Whether she'd claim the Panama money and forego Brantel's insurance payout depended on whether my description of the events surrounding Mr. Solishe's death was correct, and if she felt I could prove she killed him. If any part was wrong, she'd think I was bluffing and would try to claim the insurance money *and* the money in Panama.

"Our meeting ended with us like two wolves circling a deer carcass—the circumstances of Carlton's death—me asserting the alpha position and her wondering if she could take me down. Although we have different life experiences and genders, I felt her worldview and psychology are similar to mine and she knew I wouldn't turn her in if she took the deal. I told her if she accepted my offer she'd never hear from me again unless a future husband died under suspicious circumstances, and that I would return in a week to learn what she had decided. We did not shake hands when I left.

"Our meeting one week later, the last time I talked with her, was much different. She's an intelligent woman and decided I wasn't bluffing, so she took the low-risk option: forego the Brantel insurance claim and Mr. Solishe's exhumation, avoid a sensational and lurid trial and possible imprisonment, and walk away scot-free with over thirty million dollars from the Panama accounts. To make sure she could access the accounts, she'd already claimed her shares and transferred ten thousand dollars to her Chicago bank.

"However, before she'd sign the insurance disclaimer, she had to make sure I wasn't going to turn her in to the authorities afterwards: if I could prove she killed Carlton, why wouldn't I do it? I explained my reasons, but she's tough and denied doing anything wrong, so I focused on answering her questions. After an hour of additional reassurances and reviewing procedural issues, she signed the insurance policy disclaimer and I was able to get out of there.

Damen turned off the recorder.

"Jasper, She never asked how the insurance company felt regarding our deal—she had assumed they approved of everything, but actually I didn't share any details about our last two meetings or the deal with them until after she signed the disclaimer." Damen grinned "And I certainly don't plan on telling a living soul the vitreous I sent to Brantel afterwards was from Muffy, Mrs. Greumach's dog, that was killed a few weeks ago chasing a car when I was mowing my front lawn; I extracted the vitreous from its eyes in my garage with a syringe and large-bore needle that had been kept in my doctors bag for emergencies. What Brantel and Castelman never know won't hurt them…or anyone else.

"Rusco was hanging around as I left. He was pissed —Anita told him a few days before that she'd claimed her shares of the Panama accounts and she was planning to forfeit the insurance policy—and he threatened me. It's a good thing because I'd forgotten to give him the envelope from the hotel. As I was getting into my car, he opened it and something shocked the shit out of him…too bad."

There it is again, he thought, *the defect in my soul that allows me to judge people, and if I feel they're evil, take pleasure in their pain or demise.* It was why he had been so good in the Rangers—a cancer was in his heart—and no matter how often he had attended church and prayed for it to disappear, it remained in the background, getting better for sure, but still present. *It's what Beth saw in San Francisco...* Damen's eyes got red from emotion and he pushed the thought away.

After a few minutes, he turned the recorder back on.

"I knew 'Jimmy Kelly' wasn't the estate guard's name. That's why I sent the cup from the guardhouse to Brantel for fingerprint and DNA analysis, to find out who he really was. The fingerprints matched those of a Youngstown, Ohio, Mob punk, Frankie Cutozzo, and the DNA was identical to tissue samples preserved from the murder of a nurse in Buffalo, New York, thirty years ago. The lab contacted the New York State Investigations Division and sent a copy of the findings to Brantel's investigative team, who forwarded it to me.

"Based on the nurse's maiden name provided by the lab, I researched her obituary and it listed several 'Cirazzis' in Rochester as next of kin. Voila! Kelly turned out to be one of the killers of Mr. Cirazzi's beloved daughter whose death he mourned to me during Donny's stay in the Rochester Intensive Care Unit. The lab was unable to find a match for the second unexplained DNA sample from her body, but I suspect it was Rusco.

"The State Investigations Division contacted the FBI in Chicago to pick up Kelly, but that was the week of the terrorist attack on Miracle Mile and all FBI personnel were tied up. They didn't get to Kelly's case until the following week. By then, he had vanished.

He thumbed the recorder off.

"I shouldn't have let the Cirazzis know about Kelly, but I owe Donny's father more than I can ever repay. My own dad drilled it into me when I was a child that settling debts with friends and family is important. He also said you should do what you believe is right, even if it could land you in Hell.

"Jasper, I'm afraid my decisions during this investigation have earned me a room there."

Damen started recording again and finished his dictation an hour later.

EPILOGUE

It was a gorgeous summer morning and Penelope Liu was enjoying some perks of living in the City of Medicine and being president of Southern University. The southern magnolias around campus were in full bloom and their fragrance percolated across the campus, so she opened her office windows and turned off the thermostat. She was looking forward to a good morning—the philanthropic reserves for student scholarships and academic support would be increased and, hopefully, she'd learn more about Jack Damen's adventures with Brantel Mutual.

She received two checks this month designated for distribution into Southern's philanthropic funds per Damen's discretion. The first was from Brantel Mutual for the work he had done for them. Liu felt two million dollars was generous, but Damen spent a lot of time on the project and saved the company $20 million dollars; the 10% reward was agreed upon beforehand with Stuart Castelman, Brantel's CEO. The second check was unexpected and hand-delivered to her two days later.

Donations to Southern were usually made through the Development Office or Office of Planned Giving. However, because of the size of the gift, the donor requested that it be given in person to President Liu. An out-of-state attorney flew in that morning, met with her to ensure Damen would have discretion regarding its distribution, and presented a check for $500,000. The donor wanted to remain anonymous, and the reason given for the donation was "Dr. Damen's past services to our family."

Having been a medical researcher, Liu didn't believe in coincidences and suspected it was somehow related to Damen's work for Castelman. *I never should have asked him to do it*, she thought again, *and something horrendous must have happened for him to break down and become such a "basket case"—Damn, I'd love to know what it was.*

She told Castelman about the gift yesterday and pumped him for details about the investigation, but he was tightlipped, saying company policy prevented him from talking about it. When asked about Damen's role, he sang his praises and evaded her questions. *This is odd*, she thought, *he's usually a wellspring of information.*

Because distribution of the second check and half

of Brantel's reward, $1 million—the enticement for Damen to participate in the investigation—were up to Damen, she scheduled a meeting with him to learn which funds he preferred. She also wanted to congratulate him and share Stuart Castelman's kind words about the fine job he'd done. An added bonus would be the opportunity to ask questions about the investigation.

Damen arrived early for his appointment and was shown into her office.

"Hi, Penelope."

"Good morning, Jack. Thanks for coming by... Have a seat. I know how busy you are and I won't take up too much of your time. We need to talk about the distribution of your share of the reward money, but first I want to congratulate you on the fine work you did: Stu Castelman can't stop talking about how you saved them twenty million dollars." She laughed. "Now he thinks you fly above the water instead of walking on it... But he wouldn't tell me anything about what you did, so can you enlighten me any?

Damen's smile evaporated, "You know, just a lot of fact finding and research. Similar to how you used to look up background information for research at Palo Alto and how we clinicians investigate different possibilities when we're stumped by a patient.

A little more than that, but I'm not comfortable giving away details."

"No drama or exciting moments that you can share?"

Damen forced a chuckle and a weak grin. "Some, but not many, and I'm sworn to secrecy."

"Darn it," she teased, "you and Stuart do nothing to help out a nosey college president. But, at least I can get some satisfaction by putting money into our medical school support funds."

Liu handed him Brantel's check. "Where would you like your half of this deposited?"

Damen examined it, and in a tight voice said, "Seven hundred and fifty thousand dollars in the Elizabeth Damen Student Scholarship Fund, and two hundred and fifty thousand dollars in the Student Research Start-up Fund."

"I thought those would be the places."

She hesitated. "A second check, made out to Southern Medical Center, was hand-delivered to me by an attorney from New York City two days after Brantel's check arrived. The donor wishes to be anonymous; a letter with the check says it's for 'past services to our family.' The gift came with the stipulation that you be allowed to designate where the money is used. We don't allow stipulations with most anonymous gifts, but I reviewed it with our Board and they felt you'd know where to put it for best use." She didn't mention Castelman was not there for the discussion—the first Board meeting he'd missed in four years—or that the anonymous gift was on the agenda sent to members beforehand.

She handed the check to Damen and watched as his eyes settled on the $500,000 amount. Did his face harden or was it the light as he shifted position in the chair?

Damen said, "This is really generous."

"Any ideas who it could be from?"

"I've taken care of plenty of rich people from New York and it could be from any one of them. Or, from someone who has a bank there. I'm just happy that whoever it is decided to donate to Southern rather than buy a fancy boat or car."

She looked intently at him. "So, Jack, to your knowledge, is there anything I need to be concerned about regarding this gift? I'd hate to accept it and have Southern suffer negative fallout."

"No. I don't believe I've ever given medical care that

could be twisted into an embarrassment for the university... That shouldn't be a problem."

Liu noticed Damen's tact regarding the donor's identity, and that his answer referenced only "medical care," but she decided not to pursue her suspicions. "OK, that's good enough for me. Where would you like to see it go?"

"Into the Elizabeth Damen Student Scholarship Fund. All of it."

"Jack, a lot of students will appreciate this. Thanks from the Board, and from me, for your service and contributions to Southern." She smiled. "I know how busy you are, so I'll let you go."

Damen shook her hand and left. She walked to the window. *There's a lot I don't know about that man*, she thought, *but I like him.*

The elder Cirazzi died at peace six months after Gene Rusco's disappearance. His funeral in Rochester, New York, was attended by Mafiosi from around the country and was felt by local and national law enforcement officials to be the largest Mob gathering in three decades. Unnoticed at the funeral mass was the endocrinologist from Southern Medical Center who had been given a place among close family acquaintances. At the private reception afterward, Donny Cirazzi told Damen, "Dad hung on for years hoping to find who murdered my sister… Anything you ever need, Jack, anything, you let me know."

◆ ◆ ◆

Damen drove to Pineview Gardens Rest Home the weekend after he returned to work. He'd been able to see Beth on most weekends during the investigation but not during his breakdown and recovery at the river; however, he made sure the chocolate hearts were delivered every week.

As always, a medical assistant escorted him to Beth's room and left after he put the chocolates on her dresser and was seated. Beth was in a chair across the room wringing her hands, eyes flittering from spot to spot.

Damen said, "How have you been? I've missed seeing you, but I wasn't able to come the past few weeks because I wasn't feeling well. Now I'm back to normal."

No response.

"The staff tells me you're doing well—eating and

keeping busy, walking outside every day, and doing projects down in the Crafts Room. How do you feel you're doing?"

Nothing.

This was normal when he visited: the most she ever said was "yes" and "no," and that didn't happen often. So he talked for thirty minutes about his work and things he thought she'd be interested in, until the assistant came to show him out.

As he was leaving, Beth said, "I missed you too."

Shocked, Damen turned. Her eyes looked away.

He stumbled into the hallway, closed the door, and slumped against the wall. Tears threatened and his heart beat uncontrollably.

Someday, he thought, *maybe someday...*

ACKNOWLEDGEMENT

Throughout my life, I've enjoyed novels that could be read over a long weekend while curled up in a chair or in bed before dosing off to sleep. Adventures and mysteries are my favorites, and I envisioned how much fun it would be to write a story that others might enjoy, a story limited only by my imagination. Little did I know of the work that would be required transitioning from a background of scientific writing to creative writing or the endless hours of discipline, self-doubts and reflection, and working alone that writing a novel demands. A willingness to accept critical feedback from one's editor and other reviewers has been an additional challenge in this endeavor. After experiencing all of this and more, I have developed a profound respect for authors in all genres who've completed the writing and publishing gauntlets.

I couldn't have written this novel without the assistance of my wife, Patricia, who tolerated my daily hours of writing in isolation without complaint. She's a relentless reader and gave me feedback on every revision, always supportive but definitely constructive, and reined in my tendencies to be overly graphic in disturbing scenes and nerdy in others. We've been a team for over fifty years and I love her dearly!

A goal I had for writing this story was to collaborate with my adult children on a meaningful project, and they bought into it with enthusiasm. Distributed across North America, each with a family and several small children, they dove in and provided help as they were able: Jennifer, a speed reader whose attention to detail helped immeasurably; Lars, our business professional with an unanticipated streak of propriety, kept my medical-overboard descriptions within acceptable norms for most readers; and Elizabeth, provider of straight-from-the-shoulder feedback, brought me back to earth with comments such as "You need to rewrite the entire beginning of the novel." They and Patricia are the loves of my life and collaborating with them has given me more pleasure than I deserve.

Friends and neighbors provided encouragement whenever we discussed what I'd been doing inside our house during mornings when they were outside enjoying the weather, and their kind words meant a lot. A lifelong friend and attorney who lives several states away, Richard Hayes, shared his professional expertise as I worked to make scenes involving legal issues plausible.

Every writer benefits from having a good editor and mine, Don Weiss, was a godsend. He tactfully provided feedback and suggestions that uplifted the story, a complicated tale by a first-time novelist, into one that could be easily read and understood. I cannot overstate what an excellent communicator and teacher he was throughout the editing processes!

Kerri Flinchbaugh, a former university colleague and expert writer, gave me much-needed encouragement at the beginning of this quest, and the references she suggested I read to strengthen the foundations of my writing were spot on. Diane Taylor of Taylor Made Publishing provided valuable insights about writing and self-publishing during several educational presentations and a telephone consultation I had with her.

Writing requires support from other writers, and the Pamlico Writers Group welcomed me with open arms and made me feel at home from the very beginning of this odyssey. They are special people with a passion for improving the writing skills of others.

ABOUT THE AUTHOR

L.c. Larsen

L.C. Larsen is a retired family physician and lives in eastern North Carolina. He and his wife enjoy traveling throughout the United States and Canada with  their small trailer, visiting their children and grandchildren and as many national parks, monuments, and lakeshores as possible.

Made in the USA
Columbia, SC
26 November 2021